What on earth was Xander doing here?

And looking so incredibly gorgeous. She'd never seen him in his cowboy clothes. Dark jeans. Brown boots. A navy T-shirt. And a brown Stetson held against his stomach. *Be still my silly heart*, she thought.

"Hi. I stopped by Maverick Manor to pay compliments to the chef, and your friend AnnaBeth said you'd finished your shift, so I thought I'd stop by and tell you. Something smells amazing," he said, sniffing the air.

"I'm working on some special tofu dishes for vegan options at Maverick Manor," she explained.

"If you could make tofu smell that good, I imagine I'd pay a million bucks for a Lily Hunt hamburger."

She laughed. "You're going to give me a big head."

"You know, I could really use some cooking lessons. Even just the basics. I'll pay you well for your time and expertise."

He named a figure that was more than she made *a week*. "Seriously?" she sputtered.

"Seriously. Teach me how to make that French dip. Teach me how to make fettuccine carbonara, which I crave every other day. Teach me how to make a pizza from scratch without burning the crust."

Teach me how not to fall in love with you. she thought. She was pract

Dear Reader,

With a *very* motivated wedding planner setting up dates for the hunky Crawford brothers (one down, five to go), twenty-three-year-old tomboy, cook and student Lily Hunt doesn't expect to even be considered. But when she agrees to a blind date with one brother only to have *another* show up, the evening gets off to a mighty unexpected start.

Turns out rancher Xander Crawford isn't in the market for a wife. But Lily—the opposite of his usual type—has caught him by surprise. And when Lily becomes her own fairy godmother and Rust Creek Fall's Cinderella, will Xander be there with the glass cowboy boot?

I hope you enjoy Lily and Xander's love story—there's also lots of delicious food and two adorable senior dachshunds named Dobby and Harry! I love to hear from readers. You can find out more about me and my books at my website, melissasenate.com, and write me at MelissaSenate@yahoo.com.

Warm regards,

Melissa Senate

Rust Creek Falls Cinderella

Melissa Senate

HARLEQUIN® SPECIAL EDITION

Special thanks and acknowledgment are given to Melissa Senate for her contribution to the Montana Mavericks: Six Brides for Six Brothers continuity.

Recycling programs
for this product may
not exist in your area.

ISBN-13: 978-1-335-57400-8

Rust Creek Falls Cinderella

Copyright © 2019 by Harlequin Books S.A.

Printed in U.S.A.

www.Harlequin.com

Melissa Senate has written many novels for Harlequin and other publishers, including her debut, *See Jane Date*, which was made into a TV movie. She also wrote seven books for Harlequin's Special Edition line under the pen name Meg Maxwell. Her novels have been published in over twenty-five countries. Melissa lives on the coast of Maine with her teenage son; their rescue shepherd mix, Flash; and a lap cat named Cleo. For more information, please visit her website, melissasenate.com.

Books by Melissa Senate

Harlequin Special Edition

The Wyoming Multiples

The Baby Switch!
Detective Barelli's Legendary Triplets
Wyoming Christmas Surprise

Hurley's Homestyle Kitchen (as Meg Maxwell)

A Cowboy in the Kitchen
The Detective's 8 lb, 10 oz Surprise
The Cowboy's Big Family Tree
The Cook's Secret Ingredient
Charm School for Cowboys
Santa's Seven-Day Baby Tutorial

Montana Mavericks: The Great Family Roundup (as Meg Maxwell)

Mommy and the Maverick

Montana Mavericks: The Lonelyhearts Ranch

The Maverick's Baby-in-Waiting

Dedicated to
Marcia Book Adirim and Susan Litman.

Thank you for inviting me to Rust Creek Falls,
one of my favorite places to visit.

Chapter One

Any minute now, Lily Hunt's first blind date ever—one of the six gorgeous Crawford brothers—was going to walk through the door of the Maverick Manor hotel. Lily waited in a club chair in the lobby's bar area by a massive vase of wildflowers, her gaze going from the window to the door every five seconds. She crossed and uncrossed her legs. Folded and unfolded her hands. Slouched and sat up straight, then slouched again. Tried for a pleasant smile.

She also tried to get the better of her nerves, but she still worried that her date would take one look at her, pretend something suddenly came up, like a family emergency or a bad cough, and hightail it out of there.

Oh, stop it, she ordered herself. Even though she really did fear he might do exactly that. Lily, part-time cook, part-time student, twenty-three-year-old tomboy who lived in jeans and sneakers and had more hoodies than most teenage boys, was not the kind of woman who made a man think, *Ooh, I want to meet her.* That was more her good friend Sarah, who was gorgeous and so nice Lily didn't think it was fair. A month ago, Sarah had been the single mother of an adorable baby girl until she'd found herself falling for one of the Crawfords, ranchers from Texas who'd moved to Rust Creek Falls in July. Now she and Logan were *married.* And happily raising little Sophia together.

The Crawford brother Lily was meeting tonight? Knox. Tall, dark and dreamy like his brothers. She'd met some of the Crawford clan last month when they'd come to the Maverick Manor for dinner. Sarah had introduced Lily, and one brother was so drop-dead gorgeous she couldn't speak, which likely also contributed to why he hadn't glanced twice at her.

Confidence, girl! she pep-talked herself. Sarah had insisted on it earlier when she'd phoned to tell Lily to have a wonderful time and to call her after the date with every detail. And Vivienne Dalton, a wedding planner who'd been the one to fix up Lily with Knox, had also called to make sure she hadn't chickened out. (Yes, Lily had taken some serious convincing to accept the date in the first place.) Lily had assured Viv she was getting dressed and would be right on time at 7:00 p.m., classic date hour at the Maverick Manor. Viv had said, *Honey, I will give you only one piece of advice.* Lily had held her breath, waiting. Viv was gorgeous herself and married to Cole Dalton and ran her own successful business—a walking example of making things happen.

Be yourself, Viv had said.

That old yarn? Being herself hadn't exactly gotten

Lily very far. Granted, she had a great job as a cook at the Maverick Manor, the fanciest hotel in town. And people raved about her food, which had done more for her confidence than any appreciative glance from a guy ever could. Lily dreamed about having her own place— a small restaurant or a catering shop. Someday.

Today—tonight—was about her love life.

Two short-term relationships were all she had in that department.

She eyed the door. It was 7:00 p.m. on the nose. Lily had been there for five minutes, unfashionably early. She'd changed for the date in the women's locker room, stashing her work clothes in her locker and putting on her one good dress and one pair of heels and one pair of dangling earrings. She never wore makeup, but Sarah had suggested she try some tonight. So Lily had swiped on Maybelline mascara and sheer pinkish-red lipstick and felt like she was playing dress-up, but she supposed she was. She'd left her long red hair down instead of pulling it into a low ponytail the way she did every day.

Now 7:05 p.m. Knox Crawford was now late. Bad sign? Her stomach gave a little flop. The date clearly wasn't high enough on his priorities for him to be on time. Oh, cripes—now she sounded like her dad! Maybe she was getting antsy too early. *Calm down. Go with the flow. Sip your white wine.*

She took a sip…7:09 p.m.

Seven twelve. Humph.

Lily might not be Ms. Confidence when it came to men, but she would never let anyone treat her disrespectfully, and being almost fifteen minutes late for a date was bordering on rude. Right? Her last date was six months ago (no interest on either side) so she wasn't really up on date etiquette.

Seven fifteen.

"Lily!" came a female voice. "How lovely you look! Job interview here at the Manor? Front desk?"

Trying not to sigh as she smiled up at Maren, a woman she'd gone to high school with, Lily glanced down at her royal blue boat-neck, cap-sleeve shift dress, a cotton cardigan tied around her shoulders, and sandals with two-inch stacked heels. It worked for church and weddings, so she figured it would work for tonight.

"Actually, I have a date," Lily said, taking another sip of wine. *Waiter, bring the bottle!*

Maren eyed her up and down. "Oh. Well, have fun!" she said, tottering on her sexy high heels to the main dining room.

Lily looked around the swanky lobby's bar area at the women sitting with dates or out for drinks and appetizers with girlfriends. Skinny jeans and strappy high-heeled sandals. Form-fitting dresses. Slinky skirts. Everyone looked great and evening-ready. And here she was in her Sunday best.

Oh, Lily, get a clue already!

Seven eighteen. Her stomach flopped again, her heart heading south. She was being stood up. First time she actually "put herself out there," like her mom always told her to do, and whammo: humiliated.

She could be plopped on her couch at home with Dobby and Harry, her adorable dachshunds, eating leftover linguini carbonara and garlic bread, and instead, she was about to burst into tears. Whatever, she told herself. She'd just go home, work on a recipe, watch a movie, play with Dobby and Harry.

Just as her pep talk started making her feel better, her cell phone rang.

She didn't recognize the number but she was sure it was her date—or lack thereof. "Hello?"

"Lily, this is Knox Crawford. I'm so sorry I'm not there." There was some weird background noise as if he was covering the phone with his hand and talking to someone else beside him or something. Double humph. "Look, um, something came up and—"

Oh, did it? *Suuure.*

"And I'm really sorry but I can't make it," Knox said. "I—"

More weird background noise. Weird ocean-roar in the phone as if someone was definitely holding a hand over the speaker. Maybe he had his own female version of Davy Jones there with him. Selena Gomez or Charlize Theron, maybe.

"Hello?" a different male voice said. "Lily? This is Xander Crawford. My brother can't make it tonight, but I happen to be free for dinner and I'll be taking his place. See you in five minutes."

Uh, *what?*

"No, that's okay," she said, hoping her voice didn't sound as clogged to him as it did to her. *I am not a charity case!* The famed ire of the angry redhead? She was about to blow, people! "No worries. Bye!" She clicked End Call and stuffed her phone in her stupid little purse—she hated purses!—stood up, took another long sip of her wine, and stalked back into the kitchen, wondering how a person could feel angry and so sad at the same time.

Xander Crawford. Please. She'd seen him up close and personal and he was too good-looking, too sexy—

with a Texas drawl, to boot. She'd clam up and stammer or mumble or ramble, especially because of how weird this all was. And what was she? Someone to pity? The poor stood-up date? No thank you!

She was grateful her fellow cooks and her friend AnnaBeth, a waitress, were all so busy they didn't see her slip back into the break room. She opened her locker, and a photo of her dogs, one of her beautiful mother, and a restaurant review from the *Rust Creek Falls Gazette* that had raved about her filet mignon in mushroom peppercorn sauce with roasted rosemary potatoes and sautéed garlic-buttered asparagus reminded her who she was. Lily Hunt. She was meant to be creating magical recipes and figuring out how to get where she wanted to be in a year or two. Not trying to be something she wasn't: a woman who dated gorgeous, wealthy ranchers the entire town was vying for.

Yes, vying for. There were five Crawford brothers left and, according to Viv, their dad wanted to see them married and settled down, so he'd put the wedding planner on the case to find them the right women. All the single ladies in town had put their names in the hat, and hell, why not Lily, tomboy and all? She was flattered Viv had even asked.

And now some stand-in Crawford was showing up, probably only to save the family name since they were new in town and didn't want their dating reps to be ruined. Yeah, no thanks.

"Well, Mama," Lily said, looking at Naomi Hunt's photo, her red hair all she'd inherited from her sophisticated mother. "I did put myself out there, but it didn't work this time. Maybe next." Not that she'd agree to another date anytime soon.

She changed back into her jeans and sneakers with a relieved *ahhh*, put on her T-shirt and tied her hoodie around her waist. She wiped off the lipstick and put her hair in a low ponytail, closed her locker and headed out the swinging door into the lobby.

Right into the muscular chest of Xander Crawford.

"I'm so sorry," Xander said to the young redhead he'd just barreled into. He'd been in such a hurry to catch Lily Hunt that he hadn't considered that the door into the kitchen might have someone coming through it from the other side. Luckily it hadn't been a waiter with a tray of entrées. "Are you okay?"

"I'm fine," she said, but her eyes were like saucers and her cheeks were flushed.

Maybe it was hot in the kitchen? "I'm looking for Lily Hunt. Do you know her? She works here as a cook. Is she still around?"

The redhead stared at him, and for a moment he swore she was shooting daggers out of those flashing green eyes. "*I'm* Lily Hunt. We met last month in the dining room. I was with my friend Sarah, who's married to your brother Logan."

Oh hell. Awkward.

"I'm bad with faces," he said, which was true. "I've met so many people since we moved to Montana that my head's still spinning."

Not to mention all the women who'd introduced themselves to him over the past month. Everywhere he went there seemed to be a smiling woman, offering her card—some of which smelled like perfume—and letting him know she'd "just love to have coffee or a drink or dinner anytime, hon." At first he'd wondered if women were that friendly in every town in the state of Montana. Until he'd realized *why* women were coming at him in droves. They were coming at all the single Crawfords—thanks to his dad. Maximilian Crawford had made a deal with a local wedding planner to get him them all hitched, and that wedding planner had apparently spoken to every single woman in Rust Creek Falls.

Why was that wedding planner so raring to go? Finding *all* the eligible women in town who might be interested in being set up with a Crawford brother?

Because Max had offered Viv Dalton one million bucks to get them all married.

One. Million. Dollars.

If he and his brother Logan hadn't witnessed the exchange with their own eyes and ears, Xander never would have believed it.

Anyway, Xander had a drawer full of scented cards and had not made a single call. His father shook his head a lot over it.

Still, he was surprised he didn't remember meeting Lily. She had the determined face of a young woman who was going places. He liked it. She had freckles, too. He'd always liked freckles.

He was aware he had a smile plastered on his face. Now she did, too.

"Uh, so," she said, "like I said on the phone, no worries. Let's just forget this ever happened, okay?"

He tilted his head. "What do you mean?"

"Your brother got cold feet about our blind date and canceled. You felt bad for whatever reason and took his place. You know who I don't want to be? The woman sitting across from the guy who gave up his evening to 'do the right thing.'"

"I always try to do the right thing," he said. "But trust me, dinner with a lovely woman is hardly a chore, Lily. I'd love to take you out to dinner if you're up for it."

Her expression changed from wary and pissed to surprised. She lifted her chin. "Well, when you put it like that." She flashed him a smile, a genuine smile that lit up her entire face. For a moment he couldn't pull his gaze off her.

"You're probably wondering why I'm wearing a hoodie and sneakers on a date," she said. "I just changed back into my work clothes. I could put the dress on again if you want to wait a few minutes."

"You look incredibly comfortable," he said, tugging at the collar of his button-down shirt. "Trust me, I'll take jeans and a T-shirt over a button-down and tie any day. Luckily, as a rancher, I'm not often forced into a tie."

She smiled that smile again. "Well, then, guess we're not eating here. Unwritten dress code. And to be honest, though I love the food at the Manor, I have it *all the time*."

"Perk of the job, but I get it," he said. "Casual always works for me. I'm new around here, but I already know Ace in the Hole and Wings to Go pretty well. Either of those sound good?"

"Ooh, I'm craving chicken wings—in extra tangy barbecue sauce."

"Woman after my own heart," he said, gesturing toward the door.

She stared at him for a moment, then rushed outside as if she needed a gulp of air. "Uh, Wings to Go isn't very far." They started walking, Lily stopping to pet a tiny dog with huge amber eyes, then to look at a red bird on a branch. He liked that she noticed her environment—

and animals in particular. Xander's mind was always so crammed with this and that he'd walked straight into a fence post the other day. Two of his brothers had a good laugh over that one.

Once inside the small take-out shop, they ordered a heap of wings and four kinds of sauces. Lily got out her wallet, but he told her to put it away, that tonight was on him.

"Well, thank you very much," she said. "I appreciate that."

"My pleasure." He glanced out the window. "Given that it's such a gorgeous night, want to take our dinner to the park? We have a good hour of sunlight left."

"Perfect," she said with a smile. "And good thing my dachshunds aren't with us. Dobby and Harry would clear out the wings before we could unpack them. They'd even eat the celery on the side because it smells like chicken wings."

He laughed at the thought of two dachshunds attacking a piece of celery. He held the door open, and they exited into the breezy night air. She sure was easy to talk to, much more than he expected. Not that he'd expected anything since the only thing he'd known about Knox's date was her name. "I've always wanted dogs. Maybe one day."

On the way to the park, they chatted about dog breeds and Lily told him a funny story about a Great Dane named Queenie who'd fallen in love with Dobby but ignored Harry, who was jealous. He told her about the two hamsters his dad had finally let him get when he was nine, and how they were so in love with each other they ignored *him*. She cracked up for a good minute and he had to say, she had a great laugh.

Rust Creek Falls Park was just a few blocks away and not crowded, but there were plenty of people walking and biking and enjoying the beautiful night. Since they didn't have a blanket, they chose a picnic table and she sat across from him. For a moment they watched a little kid try to untangle the string of his kite. He looked like he might start bawling, but his mom came over and in moments the green turtle was aloft again. Xander swallowed, the tug of emotion always socking him in the stomach when he saw little kids with their moms. Big kids, too. He was always surprised at how the sight affected him. After all these years.

He turned his attention back to Lily and started opening the bags containing their wings. "My brothers and I love the food at the Maverick Manor. We're there for lunch and dinner pretty often. I'll bet you have something to do with that."

She popped open the containers of sauces. "Well, thanks. I hope so. I love cooking. And I love working at the Manor. I can try all kinds of interesting specials and the executive chef always says yes. Lamb tagine was last night's special and it was such a hit. Nothing makes me feel like a million bucks more than when someone compliments my food."

"I love how passionate you are about your work," he said. "Everyone should be that lucky."

"Are you?" she asked.

He dunked a wing in barbecue sauce. "Yes, ma'am. One hundred percent cowboy. A horse, endless acres, cattle, the workings of a ranch—it's what I was born to do."

She stared at him, her green eyes shining. "That's exactly how I feel—about cooking! That I was born to be in the kitchen, with my ingredients and a stove."

He held out his chicken wing and she clinked hers to his in a toast, and they both laughed.

Huh. Whodathought this night would work out so well? When he'd heard his brother Knox arguing with his dad earlier and then calling his date and canceling, he'd been livid. Not so much at his brother for not just sucking it up and going on the date, but at his father for being such a busybody. Knox might have gone on the blind date if he hadn't learned his dad had been responsible for it in the first place. Xander and Logan had told the other four brothers what their father was up to and to hide behind all large tumbleweeds if they saw Viv Dalton coming with her phone and notebook and clipboard, but Knox had thought the whole thing was a joke. Until Viv had apparently cornered him into going on a blind date with one Lily Hunt. He'd agreed and had apparently meant to cancel, then had put the whole thing out of his mind. Until his dad had said, "Knox, shouldn't you be getting ready for your date tonight?"

Knox's face: priceless. A combination of *Oh crud* and *Now what the hell am I gonna do?*

"What's so terrible about you going on a date?" Maximilian Crawford had said so innocently. "Some dinner, a glass of wine. Maybe a kiss if you like each other." The famous smile slid into place.

Knox had been *fuming*. "I always meant to politely cancel. I've been working so hard on the fence line the last couple days that I totally forgot about calling Viv to say forget it."

"Guess you're going then," Max had said with too much confidence.

Knox had shaken his head. "Every single woman in town is after us. Who wouldn't want to marry into a family with a patriarch who has a million dollars to throw around? No thanks."

"Well, it *is* a numbers game," their dad had said.

Knox had been exasperated. "I don't want to hurt my date's feelings, but I'm not a puppet. I'm canceling. Even at the eleventh hour. She'll just have to understand."

Would she, though? Getting canceled on when she was likely already waiting for Knox to show up?

So Xander had stepped in—surprising himself. He'd avoided Viv Dalton, the wedding planner behind the woman deluge, like the plague whenever he saw her headed toward him in town with that "ooh, there's a Crawford" look on her face. But c'mon. He couldn't just let Knox's date get stood up because his brother was so…stubborn.

And anyway, what was an hour and a half of his life on a date with a stranger? Some conversation, even stilted and awkward, was still always interesting, a study in people, of how things worked. Xander had been trying to figure out how people worked for as long as he could remember. So he could apply it to his own family history.

"Best. Wings. Ever!" Lily said, chomping on one liberally slathered in maple-chipotle sauce.

"Mmm, didn't try that sauce yet," he said, dabbing a wing in the little container. He took a bite. "Are we in Texas? These rival the best wings in Dallas."

"That's a mighty compliment. Do you miss home?"

"This is home now," he said, more gruffly than he'd meant. "We bought the Ambling A ranch and are fixing it up. We've done a lot of work already. It's coming along."

"So you and your five brothers moved here, right?" she asked, taking a drink of her lemonade.

"Yup. With our dad. The seven Crawford men. Been that way a long time."

Her eyes darted to his. "My father's a widow, too. I lost my mom when I was eight. God, I miss her."

Oh hell, she'd misunderstood about his mother and he didn't want to get into the correction. "Sorry to hear that."

"I'm sorry about your mom," she said.

Well, now he had to. "Don't be. She's not dead, just gone. She took off on my dad and six little boys—my youngest brother, Wilder, was just a baby. When I let myself think about it, I can hardly believe it. Six young sons. And you just walk away."

He shook his head, then grabbed another wing before his thoughts could steal his appetite. These wings were too good to let that happen.

Change the subject, Xander. "So what else do we have in common?" he asked, swiping a wing in pineapple-teriyaki sauce. "You have five brothers, too?"

She smiled. "Three, actually. All older. So you can guess how they treat me. We all live together in the house I grew up in—the four of us and my dad."

"Protective older brothers. That's nice. Princess for a day for life, am I right?"

She snorted, which he didn't expect. *"Exsqueeze me?* Princess? My brothers treat me like I'm one of them. I don't think they know I'm a girl, actually. I'm like the youngest brother."

He laughed, imagining the four Hunts racing around the woods, playing tag, trying to catch frogs, swinging off ropes into rivers.

"They do appreciate that I cook for them, though," she said. "And I do so because they're hopeless. I told my brother Ryan that I was teaching him to cook and that he should heat up a can of stewed tomatoes, and I swear on the Bible that he put an unopened can of tomatoes in a pot and turned on the burner and asked, 'How long should it cook?'"

Xander cracked up. "That's bad."

"Oh, yeah. He's better now. He can even crack an egg into a bowl without sloshing half on the counter or floor. It's all great practice for me for one day owning my own business—either a restaurant or a catering shop. I'm also studying for a business degree online—just part-time. But I want to learn how to start and run a successful business. I'm covering all the bases."

"Wow, impressive!" he said. "You're what, twenty-two?" She looked young. Very young. Too young for him, certainly.

"Twenty-three."

"I've got seven years on you, kid," he said. "And I'll tell you, following your passion is where it's at. I'm a big believer in that."

She sobered for a moment; he wasn't sure why, but then those green eyes of hers lit up again. "Me, too."

They spent the next twenty minutes talking about everything from the differences between Texas and Montana cattle and terrain, where to get the best coffee in Rust Creek Falls (she was partial to Daisy's Donuts but he loved the strong brew at the Gold Rush Diner), the wonders and pitfalls of having many brothers, and her favorite foods for each meal (omelet, chicken salad sandwich on a very fresh baguette, any kind of pasta with any kind of sauce). They talked about steak for ten minutes and then steak fries, thick and crispy, seasoned just right and dipped in quality ketchup.

The wings were suddenly gone but he could talk to her for hours more. They laughed, traded stories, watched the dog walkers, and she told him funny stories about Dobby and Harry. He loved the way the waning sun lit up her red hair and he felt so close to her that he leaned across the table, about to take both her hands to give them a squeeze. He truly felt as if he'd made a real friend here tonight.

But when he leaned, Lily leaned.

Her face—toward his.

He darted back.

She'd thought he was going to kiss her?

He cleared his throat, glancing at his watch. "It's almost nine? How did *that* happen?" He tried for a good-natured smile, but who the hell knew what his expression really looked like. Xander had never been able to hide how he felt. And how he felt right now was seriously awkward.

He liked Lily. A lot. But did he like her *that way*? He didn't think so. She was a kid! Twenty-three to his thirty. Just starting out. And she was the furthest thing from the women he usually dated. Perfume. Long red nails. Slinky outfits and high heels. Sleek hair. And okay, big breasts and lush hips. He liked a woman with curves. Lily was…cute but not exactly his usual type. Not that he could really tell under her loose jeans and the hoodie around her waist obscuring much of her body.

All he knew was that he liked her. A lot.

As a friend.

"Yikes," she said, that plastered smile from when they

first met on her face again. She jumped up. "Dobby and Harry are going to wonder where I am."

He collected their containers and stuffed them back in the bag, his stomach twisting with the knowledge that he'd made things uncomfortable. *Never lean toward a woman*, he reminded himself, *unless you're leaning for a kiss*.

"I live pretty close to the park, so I'll just jog home," she said quickly, tossing him an even more forced smile. "I'm dressed for it," she added. "Thanks for dinner!" she called, and ran off.

I'll drive you, he wanted to call out to her, but she was too fast. He watched her reach the corner, hoping she'd turn back and wave so he could see her freckles and bright eyes again, but she didn't.

Hell if he didn't want to see her again. Soon.

Chapter Two

The Ambling A was a sight for the ole sore eyes. Sore brain, really. Xander had thought about Lily all the way home, half wanting to call her to make sure she'd gotten home all right, half not because she might read into it.

Which made him feel like a jerk again, flattering himself.

But the way she'd leaned in for that kiss…

He would *not* lead her on.

He parked his new silver pickup and got out, the sprawling dark wood ranch house, which literally looked like it was made from Lincoln Logs, making him smile. He loved this place—the house, the land, the hard work to get the ranch the way they wanted. Xander headed in, never knowing who'd be home. Hunter, the second-oldest Crawford (Xander was third born), lived in a cabin on the property. A widower since the birth of his daughter,

Hunter and his six-year-old, Wren, needed their own space, but the girl still had five uncles to dote on her. Logan, the eldest, had recently moved to town now that he was married with a baby to raise, but he worked on the ranch, as they all did, so it was almost like he'd never left.

The place sure had changed since the day they'd arrived. They'd mended fences for miles, repaired outbuildings, cleaned out barns, burned ditches and worked on the main house itself when they had the time and energy. A month later, it was looking good but they had a ways to go.

He came through the front door into the big house with its wide front hall and grand staircase leading up to a gallery-style landing on the second floor. He saw his dad and three of his brothers up there, going over blueprints, which meant his dad had proposed a change—again—and his sons were trying to talk him out of it. There was many a midnight argument taking place at the Ambling A. When they heard the door close behind him, they all came downstairs.

"Well, well, if isn't the knight in shining armor," Wilder, the youngest of the brothers, said with a grin.

Xander made a face at Wilder and shook his head, hoping they'd go back to talking blueprints. "Lily is hardly a damsel in distress. She's very focused on what she wants. She can definitely take care of herself." The more he thought about her, about what they'd talked about, her plans, her dreams, the more impressed he was.

Logan smiled. "Sounds like the date switch was a date *match*. Knox's loss."

Knox wasn't around. He probably had left to get away from their matchmaking father.

"So? *Was* it a love match?" Finn asked. "When's your next date?"

Twenty-nine-year-old Finn was the dreamer of the group. He could keep dreaming on this one, because another date wasn't going to happen.

Lily was too young. And Xander was too jaded. She'd barely lived, and he was already cynical about love and guarded.

Xander rolled his eyes. "Get real. She's twenty-three. C'mon. And very nice."

"Ah, he used the kiss-of-death word. *Nice*," Wilder said. "Nothing gonna happen there."

That settled for the Crawford men, they turned their attention back to the blueprints. Xander scowled as they ducked their heads over the plans, gabbing away as if they didn't just dismiss a lovely, smart, determined young woman as "nice."

Oh, wait. He was the one who'd called her that.

But his brothers had stamped her forehead with the word, which meant she wasn't hot or sexy or desirable. All without even laying eyes on her.

They'd written her off.

And so did you. You're the one who put her in the friend zone in the first place.

His dad came in from the kitchen with a beer. "Ah, Xander, you're back from the date! Have you already set up a second one?"

"You don't even know if we had anything in common, Dad," Xander said. "Maybe we weren't attracted to each other."

"I just have a feeling," Max Crawford said with a smile and a tip of his beer at his son. That *feeling* should tell his father otherwise.

"I think we're just meant to be friends, Dad," Xander said.

"Meaning she's not his type," Wilder threw in. "Xander likes his women with big hair, big breasts, big hips and big giggles. All play, no talk."

His brothers cracked up.

Xander supposed he deserved that. He did like curvy blondes who didn't delve too deeply and liked to watch rodeos and have sex without expecting much in return other than a nice night out and a call once in a while. But one of those curvy blondes had managed to get inside him and surprise him, and he'd fallen hard, only to find her in bed with his best friend. The betrayal still stung. All these miles away from Texas.

Max shook his head. "You boys should give 'not your types' a chance. You'd be surprised what your supposed type turns out to be."

Logan raised an eyebrow. "If I remember correctly, Dad—and I do—it was *you* who told me that a single mother of a baby was *not* the woman for me. And she is."

"Told you you'd be surprised what your type is," Max said with a grin.

Logan threw a rolled-up napkin at his dad and shook his head with a laugh. But last month, Xander had caught wind of some of his father's arguments with Logan about dating a single mother. Max had hinted that if the relationship didn't work out, there would be *three* sad hearts—including a child who didn't ask to get dragged into the muck. Xander had known his father had to be thinking of his ex-wife and how she'd abandoned them all. Times like that, he forgave his dad for being such a busybody.

Still, Xander *was* sticking to his type, but this time,

there was no way any woman was getting inside. These days, he was only interested in a good time and he always made that clear.

Except that hadn't been clear to Lily Hunt. Oh hell. She'd thought she was going on a date in good faith, that had gotten all messed up, and then he'd stepped in to save the night—and had ended up making it worse. He shook his head at himself. Now he really did want to call her and doubly apologize, but how would *that* sound?

Uh, hi, Lily, sorry for making your night go from bad to worse when you actually thought I was leaning in a for kiss.

Getting stood up by Knox might have been more fun. He sighed.

But maybe Lily was just out for a good time herself? Could it be? She seemed a little too focused and serious-minded for that, though. Still, with her life so set on track, perhaps she just wanted a nice night out and some laughs. It was possible.

He tried to imagine Lily Hunt, with her freckles and big dreams and flashing green eyes, so full of life, out for a good time, giggling and whispering about what she was going to do to him while raking her nails up his thigh. Frankly, he couldn't. First of all, her nails had been bitten to the quick. And honestly, he didn't want to think of her in any way but as a new friend.

"Well, I need to do some research on the cattle we want to add to the Ambling A," Xander said. "See y'all in the morning." He took the steps two at the time, wanting to get away from this conversation.

Lily wasn't his type. Plain and simple. And even if she were, he wouldn't be interested in a relationship. Not anymore. Besides, he had the ranch to concentrate on and a new state to discover, not to mention a new hometown to get to know. That was enough.

Just let the night go, he told himself.

Upstairs in his bedroom, he sat at his desk and opened his laptop, fully intending to research local cattle sales. But he found himself going to the website for the Maverick Manor and looking at their lunch menu—just in case he wanted to drop in tomorrow after a hard morning's work.

"French dip au jus on crusty French bread and a side of hand-cut steak fries" was one of tomorrow's lunch specials. He'd just eaten and his mouth was already watering for that meal. Yeah, maybe he'd go to the Manor for lunch and even pop into the kitchen to say hi to Lily.

That was what friends did, right? Popped in? Visited? Said a quick hello? He'd do that and leave. That would make things good between them, get rid of all that awkwardness from tonight. They could truly be friends. Everyone could always use another friend.

But damn if he wasn't sitting there, staring at the list of the Maverick Manor's decadent desserts and thinking about feeding Lily succulent strawberries, watching her mouth take the juicy red fruit.

What the hell? The woman wasn't his type! They were just going to be buddies.

He clicked over to the cattle sale site, forcing his mind onto steers and heifers and far from strawberries and twenty-three-year-old Lily Hunt.

"Ooh, Lily, that hot Crawford cowboy was just seated at table three," whispered AnnaBeth Bellows, a waitress at the Maverick Manor and Lily's good friend. Lily had told AnnaBeth about her date with Xander so Lily knew the hot cowboy had to be him.

She almost gasped yet kept her focus on her broiled shrimp, caramelizing just so in garlic, olive oil and sea salt. She added a hint of cayenne in the last few seconds, and plated it the moment she knew it was done. Sixth sense.

According to Mark, table eight's waiter, the group was from New Orleans originally even though they lived in Kalispell now. Lily always had the waiters find out where her diners were from so she could add a tiny taste of home to their dishes. It was just a little thing Lily did that her diners seemed to appreciate, even if they didn't know why they reacted so strongly, so emotionally to their food. The other cooks thought it was a lot to deal with, but Lily enjoyed the whole process. Food was special. Food was your family. Food was home in a good way, the best way, and could remind people of wonderful memories. Sometimes sad memories, too. But evoking those feelings seemed to have a good impact on her diners and on her. So she continued the tradition.

She placed the gorgeous shrimp, a deep, rich bronze, with its side of seasoned vegetables on the waiter's station and raced to the Out door to the dining room. She peered through the little round window on the door, looking for the sexy cowboy.

Yes, there he was. Sitting by himself, thank God, and not with a date set up by Viv Dalton, which was her immediate fear when AnnaBeth had whispered that he was here.

Of course, he could be waiting on a date.

"Dining alone," AnnaBeth said with a smile.

Lily couldn't help grinning back, her heart flip-flopping. "Could a man *be* more gorgeous?"

"Yes—my boyfriend," AnnaBeth said, "even if Petey-pie has a receding hairline and a bit of a belly. He's hot to me."

Lily laughed. "And Pete's the greatest guy ever, too." Yes, indeed, Lily should aspire to a wonderful guy like AnnaBeth's "Petey-pie." Kind. Loyal. Full of integrity. Brought her little gifts for no reason. Called her Anna-Beauty all the time. Making Lily wistful.

Lily bit her lip. "Okay, why is Xander here after that awkward moment from hell last night on our not-a-date?"

"The *almost* kiss," AnnaBeth suggested, watching for the other two cooks plating, which meant she'd have to rush off to pick up. "I'm telling you, Xander was just caught off guard. He wasn't even expecting to have a date last night, right? But then he did, a wings picnic, and he fell madly in love with you but didn't expect to and now he's here to ask you out again."

Lily laughed. "I love you, AnnaBeth. Seriously. Everyone needs one of you. But life is not a Christmas movie. Even though I wish it were."

"Listen, my friend. You have to make your own magic. Just like you do with your food."

Lily watched Xander close the menu. She wondered what he'd decided on.

"Ah, time to take the cowboy's order," AnnaBeth said. "Back in a flash."

Lily watched them until she noticed her boss, Gwendolyn, eyeing her and then staring at her empty cooking station. She darted to her stove, working on another batch of au jus for today's French dip special.

In a minute, AnnaBeth was back with Xander's order.
The special.

She smiled and began working on it and four more for
other tables. But to table three's sauce she added just a
hint of sweet, smoky barbecue sauce, a flavor that would
take Xander Crawford back to Texas where he'd lived
his whole life until a month ago.

Could he be here to see her? If he wasn't interested in
her—and he sure hadn't seemed to be last night with that
not-kiss thing—wouldn't he *avoid* where she worked?

But then she thought of him and the reaction he must
get from women, and she was flooded with doubts. There
was no way Lily of the hoodie and sneakers would be
Xander Crawford's type. When she was young and girls
at school would make fun of her for being a tomboy, her
mother would always say, *You're exactly as you should
be—yourself.* That had always made Lily feel better. And
maybe Xander *liked* a down-to-earth woman with flour
on her cheek and smelling of onions and caramelized
shrimp and peppercorns.

Anything was possible. *That* was the name of the game.

She smiled at the thought, adding a pinch of garam
masala to table twelve's sauce since they were honey-
mooners who'd just returned from India. For table four-
teen, visitors from Maine, she added a dash of Bell's
Seasoning, a famed New England blend of rosemary,
sage, oregano and other spices.

Lily worked on five more entrées, her apron splat-
tered, her mind moving so fast she could barely think
about Xander in the dining room, eating her food right
now. Was he enjoying it? Did it hit the spot? Did it bring
a little bit of Texas to Montana today?

"Five-minute break if you need it," Gwendolyn called

out to her. "Your tables are all freshly served so you're clear."

"Ah, great," she said, grabbing her water bottle and taking a big swig, staring out the long, narrow window at the Montana wilderness at the back of the Manor.

"I just had the best French dip sandwich of my life," a deep voice said from behind her, and she almost jumped.

Xander! Standing right there.

"Craziest thing," he said. "I took two bites and started thinking about the ranch I grew up on in Dallas, my dad teaching me and Hunter how to ride a two-wheeler. I was a little mad at my dad earlier, and now I'm full of good memories, so he's back out of the doghouse."

"You can't be in here," she whispered, trying to hide her grin. She shooed him out the back door, the breezy August air so refreshing on her face. "So you loved the French dip?"

"Beyond loved it. It tasted like…home. I know *this* is home now, but that sandwich reminded me of Texas in a good way. And I left behind some things I'd like to forget."

Huh. Like what? she wondered. A bad relationship? His heart?

"It's a little trick my mother taught me when I was young," she said, making herself keep her mind on the conversation. "My maternal grandparents moved to Montana from Louisiana, and my grandmother would add just a dash of creole seasoning to everything she cooked here because it reminded her of the bayou. My mama was a little girl when they left the South, and she never forgot that taste, so she taught me about it. Now I try to add a little taste of home in all my orders. It's easy for the waiters to get a personal tidbit about where they're from or have just been."

He stared at her for a moment, his dark eyes unreadable. What was he thinking? "You're not an everyday person, Lily Hunt."

She wasn't sure how to take that. "Uh, thank you?"

He smiled. "I mean that in the best way possible. I'm not sure I've ever met someone like you. You have a bit of the leprechaun in you."

She narrowed her eyes at him. "Aren't leprechauns supposed to be the worst kind of mischievous?"

"Magical. That's what I meant. You've got a bit of magic in you." His voice held a note of reverence, and she was so startled by it, so overwhelmed, that she couldn't speak.

"I have to have another French dip," he said. "For the road. It was so good I feel like I should get seven to go for my brothers and dad. In fact, can you take that order?"

She grinned. "Absolutely."

"Good. Maybe they'll get off my case about last night's date and stop asking me all kinds of questions. I tried to tell them we're just friends, that it wasn't really a *date* date, since you were fixed up with Knox. But you know how brothers are."

Her heart sank to her stomach, so she wasn't capable of speech at the moment. All she could manage was a deep everlasting sigh of doom.

Why had she let herself believe a nutty fantasy that this man, six foot two, body of Adonis, face of a movie star, a man who could have any woman in this town, would go for the tomboy with red hair who smelled like onions? Why? Was she that delusional?

I love how passionate you are, he'd said more than once in the very short time they'd known each other.

She wasn't delusional. She *was* passionate about life—and love, even if she'd never experienced it. She sure knew what incredible heart-pounding lust felt like, though. Because she felt it right now. With Xander Crawford.

This is what it feels like to fall in love. And it was impossible to stop, like a speeding train, even if the object of her affection just told her "it wasn't a *date* date" and they were "just friends."

Just friends.

Get back to earth, she told herself. *Go make his seven French dips to go.*

"Well, back to work!" she said too brightly, and dashed inside, then realized she'd left him high and dry in the back and he'd have to find his way around to the front of the hotel to return to the dining room.

He'll manage, she thought as she got back to her station to prepare his order. She saw him sneak and dart through the kitchen, her heart leaping at the quick sight of him. Sigh, sigh, sigh.

"Lily, you're amazing," her boss said. "*Seven* French dips to go for table three?" Gwendolyn was beaming at her, so at least she had big love at work if not in her personal life.

Forget Xander Crawford and focus on where you want to be next year: owning your own catering shop or little café, whisking your customers away to home.

Sure. As if she could forget Xander for a second.

Chapter Three

"Am I right?" Xander asked his brothers and father as they sat on the backyard patio of the Ambling A, gobbling up their French dips. "Is this incredibly delicious or what?"

The Crawfords were so busy eating they barely stopped long enough to agree. Knox held up his beer at Xander. Hunter said he wanted two more.

"I'll tell you what *I'm* right about," his father said, taking a huge bite of his sandwich. "That you went to Maverick Manor for lunch just so you could see the pretty chef again. Admit it."

"Yeah, admit it," Finn said with a grin.

What was that old line? No good deed went unpunished? No way would he ever bring these gossips a good lunch again! "I went because I was *hungry*. So how's the roof on the barn coming, Logan?" he asked his eldest brother, hoping the others would shut the hell up.

"Logan, tell Xander instead how wonderful married life is," his dad said. "Someone special to come home to at the end of a long, hard day."

Oh, brother. Literally.

Logan laughed, finishing the rest of his French dip and taking a sip of his beer. "First, that *was* damned good. Compliments to your chef, Xan."

"She is not *my* chef!" Xander shouted.

Six Crawfords laughed. One stewed in his chair.

"Second, Dad is right," Logan said. "Finding Sarah changed my life. Nothing beats coming home to her every night, waking up to her every morning. And raising that cherub Sophia with her? I feel like the luckiest guy in the world."

Huh. Xander eyed his brother. He was dead serious, heart-on-his-sleeve earnest.

"All of you are going to be that lucky, too," the Crawford patriarch said. "You know, I had to be both mother and father to you boys. I didn't always get it right. I guess I want just to see you all settled down and happy. I want you to have everything you deserve. All the happiness."

Logan put a hand on his dad's shoulder.

"To happiness," Finn said, raising his beer. "I'm into it."

"Even Knox can't *not* toast to that," Hunter said.

Xander eyed the always-intense Crawford brother. Knox raised his beer again with a bit of a scowl. Knox had thanked him for going out with Lily in his place, then had grimaced when Max Crawford said, "Now that you're over being stubborn about it, there are a hundred more single beauties out there, Knox, ole boy."

"First of all, I'm still not going out with anyone," Knox had said. "Secondly, there probably aren't a *hun-*

dred people in this town, Dad," he'd added, and had made himself scarce until he smelled the French dips.

Rust Creek Falls was tiny, less than a thousand residents, but nine hundred fifty of those had to be single women. Or at least that was how it had felt ever since Max Crawford had announced—erroneously!—that his six sons were looking for wives.

"Xander, you should probably make a reservation at the Manor for dinner now, just in case," Max said with a grin. "Find out if your chef is working first, though."

Xander got up, tossing his wrappers in the trash can. "I think I hear one of the calves calling for me." He headed for the barn, the too-familiar sound of his brothers' laughter trailing him.

His chef. Hardly!

"Mmm, mmm," he heard his dad say as he rounded the barn. "This roast beef takes me right back to Texas. Coulda ordered it from Joey's Roadhouse, am I right?"

Xander smiled. *Told you.* He'd been taken by surprise as bits and pieces of memories had popped into his mind while eating at the restaurant. Just flickers that he thought he'd forgotten: Logan threatening a bully on his behalf. Knox telling their dad off when he thought their dad was being unfair with Xander about something. The constant runs to the grocery store for milk since six growing boys could finish a gallon after one cold-cereal breakfast. Christmas after Christmas, each boy picking a brother's name from the Santa hat to buy for, the three years in a row that he got Hunter.

His mother in a yellow apron.

Now it was *his* turn to scowl. He didn't often think about his mom. He didn't remember much about her, just maybe the thought of her. There were few pictures of

Sheila Crawford in the family photo albums; he had no idea what his dad had done with the rest of them. Max had probably stored them up in the attic, leaving just a few for the boys to have some idea what their mother had looked like. Logan, Xander and Hunter remembered her the most but even they had been too young to hold a picture of her in their minds. Somehow, Xander did remember the yellow apron. And long brown hair.

A calf gave out a mini moo and he shook his head to clear his mind. All this thinking of home and his family's ribbing him about "his chef" nicely contradicted each other. Thinking about his mother reminded him that marriage didn't work out. That even the people you could count on to love you, by birthright, could leave. Just walk away without looking back. Between that and finding his girlfriend and best friend in bed, he gave a big "yeah right" to happily-ever-after.

"Yoo hoo! Anyone home?" a very female, high-pitched voice called out.

Xander came out of the barn to find an attractive, curvy blonde, just his type, he had to admit, smiling at him as she walked over from her car. "Hi, can I help you?"

"I'm so sure you can, honey," she said, her voice lowering an octave. "I'm Vanessa and I was hoping to hire one of you tall, strong, strapping cowboys to teach me how to ride a horse. I'm a town gal, so no horse or land of my own."

Xander knew there were plenty of horse farms and ranches in the area that offered riding lessons. The Ambling A wasn't one of them.

He had a feeling this woman was here for a cowboy and had zero interest in horses, if her very high heels and short dress were any indication. But any woman in the market for a Crawford was looking for a wedding ring. So despite the fact that Vanessa was his type to a T, he'd have to sit this one out.

"Ah. We don't offer riding lessons, but perhaps one of my brothers can give you the rundown on who does."

"I'd be happy to hear it from you," she said, puckering her glossy red lips a bit.

"I'm not really one of the eligible Crawfords," he said.

She frowned. "I don't see a ring. Unless you're spoken for."

Lily's face flashed into his mind. His chef. That was weird. "Well, I do seem to be seeing someone, unexpectedly," he added, for no godly reason. Then realized that was why Lily had popped into his brain. She was his way out!

"For goodness' sake, why didn't you say so and save me the trouble of flirting?" She fluffed her hair. "Any of your *eligible* brothers around?"

He smiled and mentally shook his head. A woman who knew she wanted. Had to give her credit for the chutzpah. "Let me see if Finn knows about riding lessons. Be right back."

"Finn? I do like that name," she said, peering around.

"Hang on a sec."

He went around the back of the sprawling ranch house to find the Crawfords just finishing up. "Finn, there's a woman here to see you."

Finn perked right up. That was a line he liked. "Say no more," he said before dashing around the house.

Xander smiled. That was easy. He went back into the barn and got down to work, ignoring the giggles coming from Vanessa as Finn flirted.

A flash of freckles and determined green eyes came to mind again. He should let Lily know his family loved the French dip, too, right? She'd probably appreciate hearing that. He could stop by the Manor and say it loud enough for her boss to hear; who couldn't use a gold star at work from a happy customer?

Yeah. He'd stop by and let her know. A good friend would do that, and he had a feeling that was exactly what he and Lily were going to be: good friends. That was it. Sorry, Matchmaking Dad.

The Hunt house was a big white colonial not far from the center of town. Xander glanced up at the second-floor windows, wondering which room was Lily's. He had a vision of himself standing out here at night, toss-ing pebbles at her window to get her to come out as if they were in high school or something.

Something about this very young woman had him all discombobulated.

He shook his head to clear it and rang the buzzer on the side of the blue door. He liked the color; it was a deep-sea blue that might be interesting for the barns at the Ambling A.

An auburn-haired guy in his midtwenties opened the door. One of Lily's three brothers, he presumed. He had on a pristine Kalispell Police Academy uniform, includ-ing a cap.

"Hey, you're one of those Crawfords," the guy said, his hazel eyes intense on Xander.

"I am. Xander Crawford, specifically. I haven't bro-ken any laws, have I? I haven't been to Kalispell yet."

The guy scrunched up in his face in confusion, then glanced down at his uniform. "Oh, this. I'm on my way

to school. Not a cop yet, but I will be in a few months."
He eyed Xander, then looked behind him into the house,
then turned back. "Got a minute?" he asked. "I was hoping to run into one of you, but I'm rarely in town during
the day." He extended his hand. "Andrew Hunt."

Okay, now Xander was confused. "Pleasure to meet
you," he said. "So what can I—we—do for you?"

"I'm wondering about your overflow," Andrew said,
stepping out onto the porch and shutting the door.

"Overflow?" Xander repeated.

"I heard your father's trying to get his sons married
off and offered a wedding planner five million bucks to
get the job done. A buddy told me that since then, all the
places he goes in town to meet women have dried up.
Even at Ace in the Hole, our place to play darts and always meet a few ladies, even if we already know them,
there was *no one* there last Saturday night. Just a bunch
of guys. Man, it was depressing."

"*One* million," Xander corrected—quite unnecessarily,
but still. "And I see the problem."

"So, I was thinking, if you're on one of your dates and
it doesn't work out, maybe you could mention that you
know a great guy in the police academy and set something up for after six, any night."

Wait, now *Xander* was a matchmaker? Good Lord.
"Look, Andrew, I—"

"I know, I know. But listen. I'm about to have my act
totally together. I'm ready to settle down. And the playing field has been decimated. Your faults, dude."

Xander had to give him that. "I see your point."

"I'm just saying, if you want to mention my name
and availability to any lovely lady you're not interested
in, I'd appreciate it."

"I'm not interested in *anyone*," Xander said—quickly. "This is my dad's thing. Not mine."

"Well, just think of me, leaping over walls at the academy and studying for my procedure quiz, a forty-five minute commute each way, all with the intended goal of serving and protecting our communities one day."

Xander sighed. "I'll see what I can do. What's your type?"

"Nice," Andrew said. "I like nice. My last girlfriend? Not so nice. Pretty, but ooh boy."

Xander laughed. "Got it. Nice." He shook his head at that one. "I'll keep this between us."

"Oh, no need," Andrew said. "I've got the family on it, too, but they're no help. You'd think having a sister a couple years younger would mean lots of introductions and dates, but nope. Lily's either in the kitchen here or in the kitchen at the Maverick Manor or hunched over her laptop taking her online class. Thanks, Lily." He smiled.

"Speaking of Lily, I'm actually here to see her."

Andrew tilted his head. "Really? Why?"

Xander stared at him. "We're friends."

"Oh. Yeah, I figured you two couldn't be dating. I mean, she's *super* single, but I can't even imagine her throwing her name into the hat to land some rich cowboy. No offense."

"None taken," Xander said with a smile. He could imagine how Lily had her hands full with this crew if the other three Hunts were anything like Andrew.

"So you're on board?" Andrew asked. "With the overflow?"

"Sure," Xander assured him.

"Awesome." Andrew tipped his Kalispell Police Academy cap at Xander, then threw open the door. "Lily!" he bellowed. "Someone's here to see you!" He headed past Xander to the driveway. "Later, dude," he added amiably, jogging down to his car.

Wondering what he'd just gotten himself into, Xander watched Andrew drive off.

"Be right there!" he heard Lily call from somewhere in the house.

It was crazy, but the sound of that voice? His heart skipped a beat.

How many times had she told Andrew not to scream from one room to another? Lily was in the kitchen, working on a vegan entrée she hoped to introduce as an option at the Manor so that all their guests were covered, and she'd heard Andrew's loud voice as though he were standing right beside her.

She took off her apron and washed her hands, figuring her visitor was Sarah, whom she'd texted to mention that Xander had come in for lunch earlier and had barged right into the kitchen to see her. She'd asked if that could possibly mean he did like her *that way*, even when all signs pointed to a friendship only.

Sarah had said men often didn't know how they felt and figured it out as they went along or sometimes in one fell swoop. If *she* liked Xander *that way*, Sarah had texted, then she should go for it.

But it wasn't Sarah in the hallway. It was Xander.

What on earth was he doing here?

And looking so incredibly gorgeous. She'd never seen him in his cowboy clothes. Dark jeans. Brown boots. A navy T-shirt. And a brown Stetson held against his stomach. *Be still, my idiot heart*, she thought. His slightly long hair curled a bit at the nape of his neck, and his dark brown eyes were on her. The man was too good-looking.

Dobby and Harry were sitting on either side of him, staring up at him. Dobby was sniffing his cowboy boot. Harry was giving him the once-over.

Xander knelt down and gave each dog a pat, earning wagging cinnamon-colored tails. "Well, you must be the famous Dobby and Harry I've heard so much about. And even though you look identical, I bet you're Dobby and you're Harry."

"Name tags give it away every time," Lily said with a grin. "They can never get away with switching places like most twins."

He gave them both another pat and stood up. "I stopped by Maverick Manor to pay compliments to the chef from six other appreciative ranchers, and your friend AnnaBeth said you'd finished your shift, so I thought I'd stop by here and tell you."

Okay, granted, Lily's house was pretty close to Maverick Manor. She could walk there if her very old car broke down. But still, he went out of his way to go see her at the restaurant. Then out of his way again to "stop by" her house?

He liked her. Whether he knew it or not. Her stomach flipped—in a good way—and she had to stop herself from smiling like a lunatic.

Thank God for friends like Sarah who understood men! Crawford men, in particular.

"Something smells amazing," he said, sniffing the air.

Okay, she loved when he complimented her cooking skills. "I'm working on a tofu dish for a vegan option at the Manor."

"In cattle country? Well, if you can make tofu smell

that good, I imagine it'll be a hit. I'd pay a million bucks for a Lily Hunt hamburger."

She laughed. "You're going to give me a big head."

"Hey, maybe you could give me a cooking lesson sometime. I'd pay you well for your time." He named a crazy figure.

"Seriously? That much for one lesson?"

"Seriously. But I want to learn to make all my favorites. Teach me how to make that French dip. Teach me how to make fettuccini carbonara, which I crave every other day. Teach me how to make a pizza from scratch without burning the crust."

Teach me how not to fall in love with you, she thought. She was practically a goner.

"Lily, any more of that par-something thingie left?" a male voice shouted from upstairs. Ryan, the brother closest in age to her.

Lily smiled and shook her head. "Parfait!" she called back, even though she'd never stop her brothers from yelling from room to room if she did it, too. "And no, you four attacked it and there was none left for me."

"Sorry!" Ryan shouted back. "If you make more, make like five extra!"

"I see I'm not the only one who can't resist your cooking," Xander said. "Maybe I could observe as you make the tofu dish. Get a handle on the inner workings of a kitchen before we set up a formal lesson."

Xander Crawford wanted to watch her make tofu? "Who cooks for you guys now?" she asked.

"We take turns burning food. Logan's all right on the grill, but he moved out. We order in, pick up and go out *a lot*."

She laughed. "Well, follow me, then." She turned to

the dogs. "Dobby and Harry, feel free to go back to snoozing in your sun patch." The dogs waited a beat to see if the newcomer had a treat or rawhide chew for them, and since he didn't pull anything out of his pocket, they lost interest and walked back to their big cushy bed by the window and curled up.

"That's the life," Xander said, smiling as he followed Lily through the living room, past the dining room and into the kitchen.

She'd never been so aware of someone following her into another room before. He was so tall, so built, so *male* that she almost melted into a puddle on the floor. She was very used to being surrounded by testosterone. But this was something entirely different.

Especially so close up. Because the kitchen wasn't all that big and Xander was right beside her at the stove, his thigh almost touching hers.

Could she handle the heat? That was the question.

Xander was standing so close to Lily he could smell her shampoo—the scent a combination of flowers and suntan lotion. She wore green cargo pants, a white T-shirt covered by a red apron that read Try It, You'll Like It, and weird orange rubber shoes. Her long red hair was in a messy bun on top of her head with what looked like a chopstick securing it.

His awareness of her clobbered him over the head. He used to argue with his brothers over whether a man could be friends with a woman he found sexually attractive, and some said yes and some said no way because the sexual element would always be there and that meant there was more than friendship at work. Xander believed a man could absolutely be friends with a woman.

Since when was he sexually attracted to Lily, anyway? Just because he was noticing every little thing about her? The orange rubber shoes were hard to miss. Right? He was here to learn about tofu, something he knew absolutely nothing about.

And something he had absolutely no interest in, too.

You didn't even know she was making tofu until you were inside the house. You came here on pretense.

This was getting confusing. But an undeniable fact was that he was in this kitchen because he wanted to be around Lily. Listening to her. Talking to her. Looking at her.

He suddenly pictured her naked, coming out of the shower, all that lush red hair wet around her shoulders, water still beaded on her breasts and trailing down her stomach and into her navel. Every nerve ending went haywire and he shivered.

"Caught a chill?" she asked, glancing at him as she browned the little pieces of tofu in a fry pan. "I hate that. This morning I was making pancakes, fifty of them for the bottomless pits I call my brothers and father, and I suddenly got a chill even though I was standing right in front of a gas flame in August. Crazy."

He was hardly chilled. Nope, not at all.

Now she was talking about sesame oil and how to make the tofu crispy for the stir-fry. She was saying something about cornstarch and pepper, but he'd stopped hearing her words and focused instead on her face and body.

Granted, she wasn't curvy. Or big-breasted. Or remotely his usual type. But there was just something about her. He must be losing his mind because he thought it was the freckles. Or the green eyes. Or the wide smile.

Or the way she talked so animatedly about the difference between a wok and a sauté pan.

"Going to make tofu stir-fry for your family tonight?" she asked him, holding out a piece of the brown crispy not-meat on a wooden spoon. She brought it up to his mouth, and he looked at her, then slid his lips around it.

She flushed.

He flushed.

He leaned closer.

She…backed away. As if she'd been there, done that, and had lived to tell the tale.

"I, uh, you…have sesame oil on your cheek," he rushed to say, leaning a bit closer to dab it away. He forced himself not to lick it off his finger.

Saved. He hadn't been about to kiss her. No sir.

He had to get out of this kitchen, this enclosed space, with this woman. She was his buddy, that was all. Even if he *were* attracted to her, she was too young and had big dreams that she should focus on. He was a grumbly, stomped-on, love-sucks guy who wasn't getting over it anytime soon. She needed the male version of herself. A guy as great as she was.

Not that he wanted to think of her with *any* guy.

Oh hell. He needed to go find a Vanessa type and forget about this green-eyed, freckled, curveless chef who had him all discombobulated. Yes. That was what he needed. An airhead who wouldn't make him think, wouldn't challenge him, wouldn't stab a dagger through his chest.

"Appreciate the lesson," he said. "The Crawfords might not be ready for tofu, but I might surprise them one day."

"So how do you want to schedule the cooking lesson?" she asked, stirring the pan.

"Let me check my calendar," he said. "I'm pretty busy right now. In fact, I'd better get going. Later, buddy."

He didn't miss her face falling.

Buddy.

Cripes, Xander. You always go that step too far. Why had he added that unnecessary zinger?

Because now they both knew—for sure. They were friends. That was it.

He smiled awkwardly and then headed out the kitchen door as if the place were on fire.

Chapter Four

Buddy.

Buddy!

Every time she heard that word—in Xander's sexy voice—echoing in her head, she alternated between disappointment and *oh hell no!* She was not going to be buddy-zoned by Xander Crawford when she'd lain awake all night imagining the kiss that might have taken place in her kitchen yesterday.

The kiss that did not happen but could have. He would have swept her up into his arms like in a movie and carried her up to her bedroom—no, scratch that. He would have carried her into his silver pickup, raced her back to the Ambling A and his bedroom, and they'd have spent the afternoon making mad, passionate love and coming up with silly names for their new relationship. Xanlil. Lilxan.

Not exactly flowing off the tongue. Their "celeb" name sounded like a prescription medication.

She smiled, then sighed inwardly as she carried the tray of drinks and treats while Sarah Crawford wheeled her baby stroller over to a table way in the back of Daisy's Donuts. They were going to talk shop—translation: *men*— so they needed to be away from pricked-up ears in the small town. Luckily, there were only a handful of people sitting in the shop, mostly teenagers who couldn't care less about Lily's love life, so she planned to tell Sarah everything.

Not that there was much to tell. But she did need advice. And Sarah was not only way more experienced at relationships, she was married to a Crawford.

Sarah parked the stroller and smiled at her sleeping little Sophia, the seven-month-old beauty so sweet in her pink-and-white-striped pajamas, I Love Daddy in glittery print across the front. The pj's were a gift from Daddy himself, Xander's eldest brother, Logan, who loved Sophie as if she were his own flesh and blood. To him, she clearly was. Lily's faith in everything was always restored whenever she thought about Sarah and Logan's love story.

Two days had passed since their second awkward moment involving leaning toward each other, and Xander Crawford hadn't shown his face in the dining room of Maverick Manor or made arrangements for his pricey cooking lesson. He was clearly avoiding her. Of course, Lily could text him about the lesson, push things a little. But she was not going to chase a man who was making it clear he wasn't interested.

Blast. That was the thing. He did seem interested— to a point. And then he backed off. She wasn't getting just-friend vibes from the guy. Or maybe she just didn't know enough about men and relationships to understand what was going on here.

Maybe nothing was going on.

Please, Lordy, don't let me be one of those delusional creatures who thinks this and that when there's no there *there!*

Lily took a bite of her lemon-custard donut and sips of the refreshing iced tea, the sugary goodness that was always able to do its own restorative work on her mind and heart. Temporarily for the moment, anyway. As Sarah sipped her iced latte, Lily filled in her friend on all things Xander.

Sarah picked up her frosted cruller. "Yup, I know that advance-and-retreat well. I went through it with a Crawford brother myself. I'm telling you, Lil, it takes men a while sometimes to see what's in front of their gorgeous faces."

Lily eyed Sarah's beautiful wedding ring. "I don't know. I have all kinds of crazy feelings for Xander. *All* kinds. I think he's incredibly hot. So sexy. And he's smart. Funny. Laughs at my jokes. He loves dogs. He's passionate about his work and helping his family restore the Ambling A. Did I mention he's so hot I can barely look at him sometimes?"

"Oh, trust me, I know that well, too. The man is interested, Lily. I wouldn't say it if I didn't think it was true. Sounds to me like maybe he didn't plan on getting involved with someone, though."

"But he has a highly skilled wedding planner setting up dates for him—for all the single Crawfords," Lily pointed out.

"Ugh, that," Sarah said with a grimace. "Has Xander gone on any?"

"I don't know. I hate the thought of him being fixed up with anyone." She took a grumpy bite of her donut, even the delicious sugary confection not making her feel better this time around.

"Well, worry not, my dear. You said he asked you to give him a cooking lesson, right?"

"Right…" Lily prompted, confused by where her friend was going.

"You'll be confined to one room for a few hours, working on a few recipes together—then testing them out. A lot can happen in a few hours." She nodded sagely and took another bite of her cruller, sliding a glance at baby Sophia, who continued to snooze through Lily's man troubles.

Hey, at least she had man troubles. In the past year, she'd had one bad date. That was it.

Why? Because she was shy around men? Because she was a tomboy?

She glanced down at her jeans and blah blue T-shirt with Billy's Bait Shop and an illustration of a worm on a line. Then she looked at Sarah. A new mother. And what was Sarah wearing? A cute sundress and flat metallic sandals. Her friend looked so pretty and pulled together. What was Lily's excuse for dressing like one of her brothers?

Oh God. This shirt *was* her brother's. Ryan's.

You are hopeless, Lily Hunt. This wasn't her or her style. She'd always wanted to tag along with her older brothers and so she dressed like them to play rough like them, and it had just become her look. Huh. Maybe she needed to go shopping. And beg Sarah to come with her and play stylist.

And what? Skinny jeans and a tighter, more feminine top would suddenly make Xander Crawford fall for her? Nope. Didn't work that way. Whatever made Xander so…ambivalent about her had nothing to do with her look. She thought, anyway.

Why was this so confusing?

"Lily, if something is between you two," Sarah added, "it'll happen. Trust me."

Hope bloomed in Lily's heart. She thought about the way they'd almost kissed in her kitchen two days ago. "You are absolutely right."

The thought of something happening between her and Xander—like being in bed with him—almost had her blushing. "I might have to get a little bold." Same with her cooking. Same with working on her business degree. Same with anything she wanted. She had to put herself out there, climb out on a limb and make stuff happen.

Sarah grinned. "Indeed you might. Go for it."

The next time she saw Xander, she *would*.

She needed a new look. She needed new *moxie*. And she felt it roaring up inside her.

Xander decided that if Viv Dalton was going to set him up on dates, he might as well have some control over whom he was fixed up with. Since he'd arrived in Rust Creek Falls, he'd made excuses every time the woman had approached him. He'd see her coming toward him in town, notebook in hand, one hand in a wave, a determined gleam in her eye, and he'd tap his watch and turn in the opposite direction. Now he'd actually arranged a meeting with Viv and sat across from her in her office, watching her big smile fade with every word he said. Viv was a few years younger than him, tall and slender with blond hair in a fancy twist. Her eyes were narrowed on him as though she couldn't quite believe what she was hearing.

He'd been at it for a good five minutes. "She doesn't need to be very bright," Xander went on. "Chatty is fine, but let's keep it to small talk."

"Uh, got it," Viv said, barely able to hide the "you've got to be kidding me" expression on her face as she took notes. "So let's see if I've got this straight, Xander." She peered at her notebook. "You're looking for a peroxide blonde who knows her way around a curling iron, wears makeup and high heels, and has a 'great giggle'? Great laugh I've heard before. Great giggle is a new one."

"Look, my dad wants you to set me and my brothers up on dates that might lead to something serious. So shouldn't I let you know what I'm looking for in a woman?"

"But you're not actually looking for *anything*, Xander. If I may be so blunt."

Touché. "What I'm not looking for is to get serious," he explained. "I think it's important that you know that. I don't want to hurt anyone, disappoint anyone, lead on anyone. I'm looking to have a good time—that's it. And I know what I like."

The way Xander saw it, he could do himself and Andrew Hunt a favor. Anyone Viv set him up with who was too nice or too interesting or actually had him sharing details of his life the way Lily had within ten minutes would find her name and number passed on to Andrew.

Viv sat back in her chair and clasped her hands in her lap. "I heard that instead of Knox, *you* ended up going out with Lily Hunt. How'd that go? I'm assuming not well, since Lily is the opposite of everything you described as your perfect woman to not be serious about."

Green eyes and freckles and orange rubber shoes came to mind. Tofu. Dachshunds named Dobby and Harry. Suntan lotion and flowery scented hair.

He wondered what kissing Lily would be like. Passionate, he was sure of that. Lily approached everything with zing. Kissing her would be like having all of her. And if kissing her would knock him out, he could only imagine what seeing her naked would do to him. Where else did she have freckles?

"Xander?"

He blinked and realized Viv Dalton was staring at him. Waiting for a response. Oh God. He'd been fantasizing about Lily Hunt. What was happening here exactly?

He cleared his throat and sat up straight. "Lily is a very nice person."

"Ah, nice," she said with a nod.

He frowned. "Well, she *is* nice. She's great. Smart, full of life, passionate about her job, has big goals and dreams, loves her family, dotes on those little sausage dogs. Did I mention she's going to give me a cooking lesson?"

Viv eyed him, scanned her notes and then leaned forward. "Tell you what, Xander. I'll see who might fit the bill and text you if the right gal comes to mind."

"Perfect," he said, getting up. "No pressure. I like no pressure."

"No pressure," she agreed, standing and shaking his hand. "Good luck with the cooking class."

Was it his imagination or was there a slight gleefulness in her tone?

He wished he'd scheduled that cooking lesson for right

now. He wanted to be with Lily, talking to her, looking at her, making a mess in the kitchen with her. But hadn't he met with Viv specifically to set up dates with his type in order to push Lily from his mind? Yes, he'd done exactly that and now he wanted the opposite.

All those things he'd said to Viv about Lily were true. So of course he wanted to be around her. He liked her, plain and simple. Maybe the cooking thing was too much. Too…intimate. Yeah, it kind of was. He could put that off for a while until he understood just what he was feeling for Lily Hunt.

That settled, he decided to go pay her a visit, see if her dogs needed walking since she was so busy with school and her job at the Manor. A friend would absolutely do this.

During the next week, Lily counted five times that Xander Crawford had found a reason to "stop by." *Five* times.

Early in the week, he'd appeared at the back door of the kitchen of the Maverick Manor and offered to take Dobby and Harry for a walk since it was an "incredibly gorgeous summer day" and she was cooped up at work. That sure was thoughtful. His visit had coincided with her fifteen-minute break, so they'd stood outside in the back and chatted about the day's specials, which included homemade spicy onion rings, and how onions did not make him cry like other people, and how he preferred sautéed onions to raw on his burgers. He'd started to go, then had turned back and said he wouldn't able to schedule that cooking lesson for at least a week since he was very busy with work "and stuff" at the Ambling A. Disappointment had lodged so heavily in her chest that she'd been surprised she hadn't tipped over. Then, off he'd gone, her brother Ryan reporting fifteen minutes later that "the tall dude came by and took out the dogs and good thing because I forgot to, sorry."

The next day, Xander had texted her a hello and she'd responded with a frazzled emoji and mentioned she was stuck on a school assignment about business expenditures, and a half hour later, there he was, showing her a few pages of the financials from the Ambling A, and two hours later, everything made sense. Up in her bedroom, he'd spent two hours going over economics and finance—that had to mean *something*. She'd had to force herself to concentrate on the topic and not on the fact that Xander Crawford was sitting on the edge of her bed. She'd done a lot of fantasizing about Xander in that very bed.

The next afternoon, he'd needed a "woman's opinion on which tie he should wear to a rancher's association meeting since he was thinking of running for the board—or maybe not."

Sarah had squealed over that one when Lily texted her about it. The man is crazy about you!

Except he never "leaned" toward her again. Not the next two times he'd dropped in at the Manor—once in the kitchen to rave about the grilled tuna lunch special, or when he'd appeared right before quitting time last night because he thought she might like some company walking home. She certainly did. They'd sat on her porch, watching Dobby and Harry run around the fenced yard. He'd commented on the crescent moon and the Big Dipper, and she'd almost rested her head on his shoulder. That was how natural being with him was. How comfortable she was with him.

That he liked her wasn't in question. But he didn't look at her the way she was sure she looked at him. He looked at her the way she looked at the two male cooks at Maverick Manor. Like friends.

So...what gives?

Being buddies with a man who made you fantasize about taking off his shirt and undoing his belt was a first for Lily. She lost her train of thought midsentence when she was around him or he popped into her mind—which was constantly.

"Lily! I need your help!" came the very loud voice of her brother Andrew from the direction of his bedroom.

She sighed and put down her Economics 101 textbook. She was focusing more on a tall, dark and hot cowboy than on the difference between classical economics and Keynesian economics, anyway.

She headed two doors down to Andrew's room. She coughed as a cloud of men's body spray greeted her. Waving the air in front of her, Lily said, "Wherever you're going tonight, you're gonna need to stand outside for a good twenty minutes to let all that dissipate."

Andrew, who was all dressed up—for him, anyway, since he was either in his police academy uniform or a T-shirt and sweats—eyed his reflection in the bureau mirror as he brushed his short hair. He added a dollop of gel. "No way, sis. According to the bottle, I smell like mountain energy." He took in a deep breath and smiled. "Heidi will love it."

"Who's Heidi?"

"My date for tonight. We're going to the Maverick Manor. You working tonight? Please say yes. I need you to do that thing you do with people's food so that tonight is extra magical."

Lily laughed. "I'm not working tonight, sorry. But I'm sure your date will absolutely love you. Where'd you meet her?"

"I haven't yet. It's a blind date. Thanks to Xander. I owe the guy. He set us up."

Lily gaped at her middle brother. "Xander? How'd that happen? I didn't even know you two knew each other."

Andrew glanced at her in the mirror, then used his fingers to slightly push up the front of his hair. "We met the other day when he came to the house. I asked him if he'd talk me up to any of his dates that didn't work out, and he called me a couple days ago and said he'd met a great young woman and thought we might like each other, so he gave her my number and she called. How awesome is that?"

Yeah, awesome. Xander was going on dates. And passing on the ones who didn't warrant a second date to her brother. She wondered how many Xander *hadn't* passed on.

"Should I wear black shoes or cowboy boots?" he asked.

She glanced at his feet. "Either."

"Oh, big help!" he said. "Thanks."

The thing was, she really didn't know. She wasn't exactly a fashionista. And she hadn't exactly gone on a lot of dates to know what guys wore. Xander had been wearing expensive-looking black shoes on their not-a-date, but his pants were dressier than Andrew's dark gray chinos. "Go for the shoes," she suggested.

He nodded. "I think so, too. The Maverick Manor isn't exactly the Ace in the Hole."

She dropped down on the edge of his bed. "So...what did Xander tell you about Heidi?"

"Just that she was very nice and he thought I'd like her."

"Nice?" she repeated.

"Nice. That was my one request."

Huh. That was a surprise. "I thought guys wanted pretty and hot and fun."

"Some guys, I guess. I'd be happy with all that. But what's the point of hot if she's a royal PITA?"

Lily laughed. "Good point."

Andrew put on his black shoes, glanced at himself one more time in the mirror, said "Wish me luck" and then raced downstairs before she could say another word.

She wondered why the date with nice Heidi hadn't worked out with Xander. Duh, she realized. Because Heidi was nice. And Xander obviously didn't go for nice. A man like Xander Crawford, who could have any woman in town, would want hot. Maybe nice, too, but hot.

Exactly what *she* wasn't.

She groaned.

Whatevs! she screeched at herself. Hot wouldn't get her her own gourmet café or catering shop, now would it? Hard work would. Brains would.

She sighed and trudged back to her room. As she flopped onto her bed next to her econ textbook, her heart sank so low she thought she might crash through the bed onto the floor.

Her phone pinged with a text.

From Xander.

She almost didn't want to read it. How had she gotten his small attentions all week so wrong? She'd really thought there was something brewing between them. But they really and truly were "just friends."

She stayed flopped on her back and read the text.

This might be too short notice, but I'd like to hire you to cook a special dinner for my dad and brothers on Saturday night. We finished repairing a tough line of fence and I'd like to celebrate with a family party. I'm thinking 7:00 p.m. for dinner. We're all pretty much meat-and-potatoes kind of guys, but I'll leave the details up to you.

Saturday night. Two days from now. Hell yeah, she was available. But what was the point? To fall even harder for a man who wasn't remotely interested?

Still, they *were* friends. And he was asking for her help. In fact, he was offering her another paying gig— and if she wanted to take two courses next semester, she could use the extra money.

I'm in! she texted back ever so breezily when she felt exactly the opposite. And thanks, she added.

Thank YOU, was his response.

If only there was a magic spice or ingredient she could add to the food to make Xander Crawford fall for her.

Okay, she couldn't help it. C'mon, how could she? Of course Lily found an excuse to hustle over to the Maverick Manor to check out this Heidi who was too nice for Xander Crawford. She was sure Heidi would be a plain-Jane type like her. Then she'd know that it wasn't her so much as her look that didn't attract Xander, and maybe she'd feel better.

It's not you, it's me. It's not me, it's you. Who the hell knew?

Big sunhat pulled down low, red hair tucked up under, Lily dashed into the Manor and stood behind the giant vase of wildflowers. She glanced around the lobby for her brother. No sign of him. She was glad there was no sign of Xander, either—on a date with another woman.

She dashed into the kitchen and peered through the Out door into the dining room.

There. Table eleven by the window. Her brother was smiling and chatting. And facing him was…America's Next Top Model.

Or close to it.

What? This was Xander's "it didn't work out but she's nice"? Heidi was tall and busty, Lily noted, wearing a pretty yellow sundress with a flounce near her knees. She had on high-heeled sandals. And if Lily wasn't mistaken, sparkly baby blue toenails. She also had long honey-brown hair in perfect beachy waves.

Lily watched as Heidi laughed at something her brother said and reached over and touched his arm. Andrew could not look happier.

If this woman wasn't Xander Crawford's type, then who was? Certainly not Lily Hunt.

It was time to give up on him. Cook his family dinner for the celebration, teach him to cook those three favorite dishes, make some money for her future and then move on.

"Lily? Someone called you?" her boss, Gwendolyn, said, rushing over to her. "Great! If you could whip up three filets, subbing the baked for the rice pilaf, that would be great."

Before Lily could say a word, Gwen, wearing her frantic expression, was heading over to Jesse Gold's station, but the cook was nowhere to be found. Gwen flipped a filet mignon and poured béarnaise sauce on it, letting the flames sear it. "Jesse was turning green and almost fell over, so I sent him home. We're booked tonight, so even me pitching in here won't be enough."

"I'm on it," Lily said, whipping off her hat and declaring the filet done and plating it.

This was good, actually. Being so busy would keep her from thinking about Xander and his horde of dates. Beautiful dates.

"Hey, Lily!" AnnaBeth said with a smile as she came in from the dining room. "Your brother's here on a hot date. He's having the filet special, she's having the lemon sole. Oh, and she's from South Dakota, by the way. Gonna work your magic on her fish? Is South Dakota famous for anything?"

Lily immediately thought of chislic, like shish kebabs but without the vegetables. Just delicious little chunks of salted meat on tiny skewers. They hadn't ordered appetizers, but she'd make up a small dish of chislic for them from a filet mignon that Gwen said had ended up searing too long when Jesse had been distracted by not feeling well.

She worked fast and had a little plate ready in no time. "Here," she told AnnaBeth. "You can tell table eleven this is compliments of the chef."

"Ooh, that looks delicious," AnnaBeth said.

Lily smiled and got back to work, starting on Heidi's sole now that her brother's filet was at the rare mark. By the time the sole was done, the steak would be perfectly medium.

"Uh, Lily?" AnnaBeth said, rushing over with the plate of chislic. It was untouched. "Your brother's date took one look at this and said 'Excuse me,' and ran out of the dining room. I think she might be in the restroom."

"Oh no. The dish upset her?"

AnnaBeth bit her lip. "I think so."

Lily plated the entrées and then dashed to the window on the door, AnnaBeth on her heels. Her brother looked worried. He kept glancing toward the arched doorway that led into the lobby.

Oh God. Had she ruined their date? Had "home" brought up bad memories for Heidi?

She had to get back to her station and work on her orders. She had another waitress with four tables that had recently been seated, and she needed to be on point.

They raced back over to Lily's station, AnnaBeth putting the two dishes on the elegant serving tray. "I'll try to find out what's happening."

Lily didn't add her special ingredients to the next three tables of orders she'd received from Holly, the other waitress in Lily's section. Maybe she should mind her own business. She shouldn't even be here at all. Now thanks to her nosy ways, she'd wrecked her brother's date when it had clearly been going very well.

She made two of the special pasta entrées, got three more filets going and two more lemon soles, forcing herself to focus on her work and not her urge to rush back to the little window to see if anyone was still at her brother's table.

AnnaBeth came back into the kitchen with her empty tray.

"Is the food just sitting out on the table getting cold?" Lily asked.

AnnaBeth smiled. "Nope. In fact, come take a look."

Lily's eyes widened and she rushed back over to the window. Her brother and Heidi now sat side by side at the round table instead of across from each other. Heidi was holding up a piece of her lemon sole to her brother's mouth, and he took the bite. Heidi then picked up her napkin and dabbed Andrew's lips, and then they both laughed and held each other's gazes.

She had no idea what had happened, but she was glad it had!

Lily's phone pinged with a text. Probably Xander canceling on hiring her for the party.

She glanced at her phone on the counter. No—the text was from Andrew. Her brother had practically typed a novel.

Heidi's freshening up in the restroom so just a YEEHA! that you ended up working tonight and made that little SD appetizer for her! Turns out her mom died last year and always used to make chislic every Sunday for family dinner. She got all emotional and excused herself but I found her in the lobby and told her about Mom passing and how Dad still makes her crawdaddy mac and cheese and corn bread every Sunday for us, even though his corn bread is awful, and how we feel her with us. We talked about our moms for a while and then it was like we'd known each other forever. We're going out again tomorrow night! You rock, Lil. Don't know how you do it but I'm glad you do.

Huh. She sent back a heart emoji, her own heart bursting with happiness for him and for herself, since she hadn't ruined his night after all. Au contraire.

At least one Hunt's love life was going in the right direction.

Chapter Five

Xander had exhausted his excuses for checking to see if Lily "needed help" during the past hour that she'd been in Ambling A's kitchen. She'd let him help make the béarnaise sauce for the filet mignon, which had smelled amazing, and also peel potatoes, which he'd found less fun, and then she'd shooed him out to be with his family.

Something was different between them, he thought. She was being kind of…distant. Treating him as if he were a client instead of… Instead of what? Someone she was close to?

A friend?

Why couldn't he seem to get a grip on where he was with Lily? He should be happy she was treating him like a client instead of a crush—if that was what he should call it. In the past week, hadn't he gone out with three women, one set up by Viv Dalton, two who'd asked him out in town, to restore order to his head?

And despite making it clear to Viv that she should set him up with only airheads who giggled, she'd arranged a date with a perfectly nice, intelligent, interesting woman named Heidi whose family had moved to Montana from South Dakota last year. They'd had a lot to talk about, and she'd looked a little surprised when he'd said at the end of the date that he was going to be honest and tell her he wasn't looking for a relationship with anyone and that he knew a great guy who was, if she was interested. Heidi said she trusted his opinion, and voilà, she and Lily Hunt's brother Andrew were on date number three right now, third night in a row.

The other two women he'd gone out with had been more his type. One giggled even when she'd backed her car—she'd insisted on driving since she had a little two-seater she liked zipping around in—into the sheriff's SUV. Then she giggled as the sheriff, who didn't look remotely amused, gave her a Breathalyzer test. They hadn't had an ounce of alcohol to drink at that point, but afterward, Xander could have used a few bottles of whiskey to get through the next hour of dinner. He'd turned down her suggestion of a nightcap in her condo, seen her safely home and then walked back two miles toward town, where luckily his brother Wilder had been passing by in his truck and given him a ride back to the ranch. Man, had Wilder had a good laugh all the way home.

Xander had wanted to cancel the next night's date, but then he remembered how he'd refused to let Lily get canceled on, so he'd forced himself out with Dede, who was the cheerleading coach for the high school and had a bad habit of screaming "Whooooo!" whenever she was excited about something, holding her arms straight up in the air and shaking imaginary pom-poms. She wasn't an airhead at all, it turned out, and luckily, she'd ended the date early, sobbing that she'd only asked him out to make her ex jealous and they'd walked right past the guy in the restaurant she'd known he'd be eating in with his family and he hadn't even blinked.

Dating and relationships sure were hell.

"Go on," Lily said now, making shooing motions with her hands. "I'm fine in here. It's my habitat, remember?"

He nodded and smiled but wanted to stick around. Find out what she'd been up to the past few nights since he hadn't gotten a chance to pop in on her. But her focus was on the heap of steaks and potatoes and asparagus smelling so incredible.

Go, he ordered himself, everything in him resisting leaving the room. "Holler if you get lonesome in here by yourself."

"The kitchen is the one place I never feel lonely," she said, locking eyes with him.

He held her gaze, something—hell if he knew what—spinning up inside him. He couldn't move his feet, couldn't look away.

But then she was shaking the pan with the asparagus, and turning down the burners on the steaks, and he took one last good look at her profile, the freckles on her nose and cheeks, before slipping out, his chest heavy.

The laughter and loud chatter in the living room grabbed his attention as he headed in, the Crawfords all congregated for the party to celebrate another piece of the Ambling A coming together, becoming home.

Hunter sat with his six-year-old daughter, Wren, on his lap, her long blond hair in two of the most crooked braids Xander had ever seen. Hunter had been mother and father to his sweet little girl since Wren was born, and Xander had to hand it to him for doing such a great job. He braided hair and packed day-camp lunches, and stayed up all night when Wren was sick or had bad dreams. The guy had a lot on his shoulders. Sometimes Xander wondered how *he'd* do as a father—not that he had any plans to become one anytime soon.

It was crazy how even when you picked the right woman, as Hunter had done with his late wife, your whole life could go belly-up. It was a sober reminder that Xander was 100 percent correct not to get serious about a woman.

Sharing the big couch with Hunter and Wren were Logan and Sarah, Sarah playing some kind of clapping game with her adored niece. Finn was deep in conversation with Wilder in the two club chairs across from the love seat where Xander sat with Knox, who was deep in thought—as usual. Meanwhile, his father sat in his space-age recliner with features that turned on lights and the television, and massaged his back and neck.

"Well, Crawfords," Max said with a drawn-out shake of his head, "I must say I'm disappointed to see that there's only one lovely woman joining us for dinner tonight. By this point, I expected at least half of you to be seriously involved."

"Can we not alk-tay about this in front of En-Wray," Hunter muttered through gritted teeth, nodding his head at his six-year-old daughter.

"I know pig latin, Daddy," Wren said with a grin.

Xander laughed. "And there are *three* lovely women at the table tonight, so there's your quota, Dad. Sarah, baby Sophia and Wren."

His father's gaze moved from Logan's wife and baby to Hunter's little girl, and he grinned. "I stand corrected. But still!"

"Don't you mean *four*?" Sarah asked. "Isn't Lily joining us for dinner?" She glanced around at faces but lingered on Xander's.

"Of course she is," Max said, slapping his knee. "That talented chef did all the hard work—she should get to sit down and relax and enjoy her own masterpiece."

"I agree," Sarah said with a smile. "In fact, I'll go put a place setting out for her. Be right back."

Seat her next to me, Xander wanted to tell Sarah, but of course he couldn't. He watched her dash into the kitchen.

Five long minutes later, Lily came out of the kitchen holding a platter of steaks that smelled so good everyone went silent for a moment. Sarah was right behind her with a tray of big bowls holding roasted potatoes and asparagus. Xander hopped up and asked if he could help bring anything out, but Lily smiled and said this was everything.

Then she glanced around and looked kind of uncomfortable and said, "Sorry that I'm not exactly dressed for a dinner party. I really just expected to be in the kitchen, not joining you."

"What?" Max said, eyeing her. "You look just like the rest of us. One of the boys."

Oh, Dad, Xander thought. *Enough with the asides.*

Lily bit her lip and awkwardly smiled, shifting a glance to Sarah, who was casually dressed but not quite to the degree Lily was. Lily wore a red scoop-neck T-shirt with a white apron over it, loose jeans and blue sneakers, her red hair back in a ponytail.

Luckily everyone else was focused on the aroma and platters and trooped into the huge dining room, Max taking his place at the head of the long farmhouse table. Xander took a seat down at the other end to avoid any marriage-oriented conversation his father might start up. Logan and Sarah sat across from him, baby Sophia sleeping in her carrier on the hutch along the far wall.

Lily took a seat right beside him.

"First, a toast," Max said, raising his wineglass. "To the Ambling A and all the hard work you boys have put into turning this place into a home. I couldn't be prouder of you. I'll include myself in there, since I'm out there busting these old bones every day, too."

They all laughed and raised their glasses, clinking.

"And thank you to Lily, our chef for the evening, for this amazing dinner," Max added.

There was more clinking.

"My pleasure," Lily said. "Well, everyone, bon appétit!"

Platters and bowls were passed around, everyone commenting on how good everything looked.

"Oh, and Lily," Max said, "I have to apologize for my son Knox and all that brouhaha with your date. But it looks like things worked out just fine. I mean, here you are, sitting next to Xander at a family dinner." He winked and loaded his plate with potatoes.

"Really, Dad?" Knox said with a shake of his head. "And no need to do my apologizing for me. I spoke to Lily privately in the kitchen right after she arrived."

Xander had noticed Knox go into the kitchen and come out a couple minutes later. He'd figured his brother was making amends.

Lily's cheeks were as red as her T-shirt. "Xander and I are just friends."

"Just friends," Xander seconded.

"Ah, so we can talk about all the dates you went on this past week," Wilder said. "Any work out?"

"Come on, Xan," his father said. "Tell me you have one *second* date."

Was it his imagination or was Lily pushing her potatoes around on her plate, her expression both grim and forced pleasant?

"Let's leave Xander's private life to himself," Sarah said. "You boys. Seriously!"

"Yeah, let's listen to Sarah," Xander agreed, wanting to hug her.

"Fine, fine," Max said. "Now, Lily, I hear you have three brothers, so you're used to all this testosterone."

Lily laughed. "Definitely."

The conversation thankfully turned to stories about the Hunt brothers and the Crawford brothers, both matched for mischief.

"Oh, Lily," Hunter said. "I'm really sorry but Wren and I won't be able to make your kids' cooking class tomorrow afternoon. I forgot I promised a friend I'd help him move. Wren was really looking forward to it."

"Aww," Wren said, looking pretty sad. "Now I won't know how to make tacos."

"Well, I'll be hosting more kids' classes," Lily assured her. "The next one is for kids a bit older than you, Wren, but I'll have another one for your age group in September. That's just a month away."

Xander recalled Lily mentioning she taught cooking classes at the town rec center, but he hadn't known Hunter and Wren signed up. "Why don't I take my niece to the class?" he said. "I'm free tomorrow afternoon. And then I get to spend some time with my favorite six-year-old."

And Lily, he thought.

"Yay!" Wren said. "I want to learn how to make tacos! I love tacos!"

"Perfect," Hunter said. "Thanks, bro."

Xander nodded back.

Lily sent him an awkward smile. Why was everything like that between them? Awkward and hesitant? Something was up. But what?

"Lily, I don't know where you learned to cook like this," Max said, "but thank God you did. Amazing."

There were murmurs of agreement and the conversation turned to favorite meals, then Lily brought out dessert, which were mini chocolate tarts, and suddenly dinner was over, and Lily was in the kitchen again.

Xander grabbed a few empty platters and took them into the kitchen, hoping no one would do the same. Lily stood at the sink, scraping pans.

"We'll clean up, Lily," he said. "Don't even worry about all this."

She whirled around with a grin. "Really? First the cook gets invited to dinner and now I don't have to wash pots and load the dishwasher? I'm not usually this lucky."

"Trust me, you especially deserve not to clean up with my dad getting all personal like that. Sorry."

"No worries. I'm well used to dads and brothers ribbing on me." She put the pans in soapy water to soak. "So...sorry the dating isn't working out. Though I guess that's good for my brother. I think Andrew is totally in love."

"Glad to hear it." He wanted to tell her he wasn't dating to find a serious girlfriend, let alone a wife. But was he supposed to blurt out the truth: that he was speed dating to remind him what he was and wasn't looking for?

Not looking for: Real. Serious. Even close to forever.

Looking for: A hot kiss or two. More if the woman was looking for the same and nothing else.

The reality was that Lily Hunt in her T-shirt and ponytail and blue sneakers, with sauce stains on her shoulder, was keeping him up at night by just being *herself.*

Lord. Was he falling for Lily? That was impossible, right? She was seven years his junior and looked like any number of his buddies' kid sisters in her hoodies and jeans.

He wasn't falling for her. He just liked her. That was all. When was the last time he'd met someone and developed a real bond, a real friendship? A long time ago. He just forgot what it felt like, and it was confusing because it had happened with a woman.

Hadn't he said women and men could be friends? Yes, they could.

Case in point: him and Lily.

"Well, we'll see how the dating goes this week," he said. "Viv has three more set up for me and that's just the first half of the week."

Her face fell. Just for a second. But he caught it. She had feelings for him—he knew that. And it was better not to play with her. He was telling the truth about the dates, and she should know so that she wouldn't hang any hopes on him.

If he hurt her, disappointed her, made her think something more could go on when it couldn't…he'd never forgive himself.

She was so young. She had her entire life ahead of

her. Practically all her twenties. And big dreams to fuel her. She didn't need some cynical guy already in the next decade of life.

She gave him a tight smile. "Good luck, then." She darted past him into the living room with him trailing her, said good-night and thank you to everyone, and then beelined for the door. Xander almost wished car trouble on her so he could drive her home, but her little silver car started right up.

Leaving him staring out at the red taillights disappearing down the drive.

"Jeez, just admit you've got a thing for her," Logan whispered as he came up behind him.

"What?" he said. "Of course I don't. She's twenty-three, for God's sake. I'm *thirty.*" And he was done with caring about a woman, with thinking about the future beyond a couple days. He saw where that had gotten him.

"Whatever you say, bro," Logan said with a smile and a head shake. "In due time. In due time."

"Meaning?"

Logan laughed and looked over toward the living room, where his wife sat on the sofa, lifting their baby up and down and kissing her on the cheek.

"Now you have me married with a baby?" He huffed away to get a beer, Logan's laughter trailing him.

By the time Lily pulled into her driveway, she'd burst into tears three times and had five text messages waiting for her from Sarah.

Told you he has feelings for you! her friend wrote. Taking over for Hunter at the kiddie cooking class? She added a few heart emojis and a chef hat emoji and Lily burst into tears again.

I'll believe it if he ever kisses me, she typed back. Until then, I'm operating under the assumption that he likes me as a friend.

Three dates set up this week. All before Wednesday!

She headed inside the house to find her dad home alone, Dobby and Harry beside him on the couch, a bowl of popcorn on the other side of him. He was watching a *Law & Order* marathon on cable. He took one look at her expression and put the popcorn on the coffee table and patted the space where it had been.

"Come watch, Lil. Did you know identical twins have the same DNA and one could be convicted for the crime his twin actually committed?"

"I don't think I ever thought about it before, Dad," she said, plopping beside him. Dobby came over and settled in her lap, and she stroked his soft ears.

"Everything go okay at the Crawfords'?" he asked.

The food: yes. The company: yes. Her heart: no. "Yeah," she said, unable to disguise the weariness in her tone.

"You like that tall one with the brown hair, don't you?" her father said.

She stared at her Dad. "They're *all* tall with brown hair. But how'd you know?"

He pointed the remote at the TV and shut it off, then turned to her. "Because you're my baby girl. And trust me, I never forget that. You might think I treat you like one of your brothers, but that's because I've always tried to treat you all the same. But you're the only female in the house, Lil, and you might think you hide your emotions like we try to, but you're bad at it."

Lily laughed, but tears stung her eyes. "I'm falling in love with someone who thinks of me as a friend."

"I wouldn't be too sure," her dad said. "Sometimes it just takes a while for us lugheads to know our own minds. Did I ever tell you how I thought of your mom as just a friend when we first met?"

"What? No way. You always said it was love at first sight."

"More like love at third sight," he said with a smile. "Your mom was so pretty and sparkling I didn't think I had a chance. So I didn't even give her a romantic thought in my mind. But then I got to know her and fell in love whether I liked it or not."

Lily laughed again. "You fell in love against your will?"

"Sort of. I didn't think she'd ever return my feelings. But she did."

Lily always loved hearing about when her mom and dad met. "Well, I don't think that's going to happen here. I look like a boy with long hair."

"Xander may see much more than that," her father said. "As I always say—don't rule anything out till you know for absolute sure you should."

Dobby licked her hand, which still had the faintest residue of filet mignon no matter how much she'd scrubbed.

"Thanks, Dad," she said, leaning her head on his shoulder.

He gave her shoulder a pat and then put *Law & Order* back on, the identical twin—who hadn't even known he had an identical twin—insisting he was innocent.

She wasn't in the mood for TV right now but she needed something to take her mind off Xander Crawford and her lack of a love life. Plus, it was nice to spend time with her dad. Real time. She'd opened up tonight and she hadn't done that in a long time. Sometimes Lily felt like she was changing every few seconds, new experiences hitting her left and right.

Dobby licked her hand again, and she hugged him to her, the warm little dog like a soothing balm.

After the show, Lily hugged her dad, too, and thanked him for listening—and for the good advice—then headed upstairs. She took a long, hot shower, changed into her comfiest pj's, and then got into bed, tossing and turning for what felt like hours, but when morning came, she felt well rested. Talking to her dad had definitely helped.

Don't rule anything out till you know for absolute sure you should.

Xander had pretty much confirmed she should rule him out when he mentioned his dating schedule. Right?

But he'd also made a point of seeing her later today by taking his niece to her cooking class. *Duh, because you're friends.*

She would never get to the bottom of this at this point.

She stood in front of her bureau, staring at herself in the mirror. On the dresser was a photograph of her mother—beautiful, sophisticated Naomi Hunt. She wore a sleeveless dress, dangling earrings, her hair wavy and loose around her shoulders. She'd lost her mom when she was eight, and her dad and brothers had raised her. She'd wanted to be just like Andrew, Ryan and Bobby, and so she'd never worn dresses or pink or played with dolls. And it had probably been a little easier on her dad not to have to learn to braid her hair or take her clothes shopping or paint her toenails, so he'd let her be.

And now this was what she looked like: one of her brothers. Except even her brothers had more style than she did.

Maybe it was time to change her look—just a little. Wear something besides T-shirts and jeans all the time. Learn to put on mascara without looking like a raccoon. She didn't even own perfume.

She wondered if Xander would be attracted to her if she was a little more girlie. But the problem with that was then it would bother her that artifice had gotten his attention instead of the real her.

She flopped herself down on her bed. How she wished her mama was here to talk with about this stuff.

Not that her father hadn't done a great job last night, she thought with a smile.

She heard one of the dogs scratching at the door and she opened it, and Dobby and Harry jumped on the end of her bed and curled up with their satisfied little sighs.

"We'll see," she told them. "Lots to think about. Maybe I'll even talk it over with you two."

Dobby eyed her, but Harry was already snoring.

Chapter Six

Most Sunday afternoons, Lily taught a cooking class for kids. For the summer, she also offered two workshops for older kids, which met for an hour every week on her three days off. Today was a one-day seminar for five- to eight-year-olds, which a parent or caregiver needed to attend, as well. She adored working with the young cooks.

She scanned the registration list. She had six students—her maximum so that she'd be able to give them all attention—including Wren Crawford. As the kids and their adults arrived in the rec center kitchen, Lily forced herself to stop thinking about Xander and to focus on the class. So far, everyone was here except for the Crawford duo. There were two dads, one with a daughter, one with a son. And three moms, two with daughters and one with a son. Lily checked them all off on her list, kneeling down to say hi to each of her students and handing them their special orange apron that they would take home at the end of class and could decorate with fabric markers.

She couldn't help but notice how nicely dressed two of the three women were. Granted, one was in a T-shirt and jeans like Lily, but the other two looked so polished, one in a flippy cotton skirt and ruffly tank, the other in a blue sundress.

Lily glanced at her jeans and blah sneakers. Granted, she was about to get salsa all over herself, but wasn't that what an apron was for? Ina Garten and Nigella Lawson didn't wear T-shirts to cook in. Why should Lily?

You're not one of the Hunt boys, she told herself. *You're you. Lily. And you've never really figured out what expressing that means—aside from cooking.*

She sure liked Layla Carew's pale blue cotton sundress with the embroidered hem. The woman looked pretty and comfortable and summery. Who said Lily couldn't wear something like that?

No one.

"Is this it?" Layla asked suddenly, looking around. "I thought Hunter Crawford signed up for this class."

"I thought so, too," Monica Natowky added. Monica—wearing the flippy skirt and lots of bangles on her bare, toned arms.

Lily sighed inwardly, her gaze going to their ring fingers. Empty!

Were they here for the kids' class? Or to land a Crawford?

She glanced at the third woman's finger: gold band. And what had Darby Feena come to the kids' cooking class wearing? A T-shirt and jeans. Normal, appropriate wear for the activity!

Still, it would be nice to not always be mistaken for a

nanny or a student herself. When Layla had first arrived, she'd gone up to Monica to introduce herself, thinking *Monica* was the teacher.

Ugh. Lily had no time to be thinking about her wardrobe issues. She had a class to get started.

Right then, Xander came in, holding Wren's hand, and Lily wanted to tell him to drop off Wren and leave. Who did he and his brothers think they were? Their single status and gorgeousness were causing a scene all over town, making women act like idiots. Including her. Please!

And boy, did he live up to every bit of that gorgeousness. He wore dark jeans and a green henley shirt, his shoulders so broad and his hips so slim. Lordy, Lily could look at him all day.

"Hi, Hunter," Layla trilled with a toss of her blond curls behind her shoulders. "I'm Layla and this little nugget is Mia."

Lily was about to introduce Xander and Wren to the group when Monica practically knocked her out of the way to rush over to shake his hand.

"Hunter, it's *so* nice to meet you. I'm Monica, and this is my darling nephew, Jasper. Jasper wants to be a rancher someday, too. Don't you, Jasper?"

"Yup," the cute little boy in the Western shirt and cowboy hat said.

Xander looked at both of them as if they were from Mars. "I'm not Hunter. Sorry."

Their gazes went right to *his* ring finger.

"Oh, no apologies necessary!" Monica said. "You must be one of this li'l angel's *uncles*, then."

Oh, brother. Had these two women *really* found out that Hunter Crawford had registered for the course with his daughter and signed up for that reason? Xander gave her a sheepish kind of smile as if he was so innocent. Humph!

Lily broke up this display of ick by announcing it was time to get class started. Monica frowned and darted back to her space. Each student and adult shared one table where Lily had set up bowls of precut veggies. In the first row there was an empty table next to one of the dads; Xander chose that spot instead of the free table beside Monica and in front of Layla. She could practically hear them sigh with disappointment.

"Welcome!" she said in her loud, kid-friendly voice. She stood behind a table full of bowls and her electric hot plates. "I'm Lily Hunt, your cooking teacher for today. Guess what we're making?"

"Tacos!" lots of happy voices shouted.

"That's right. We're making vegetarian tacos. Who knows what vegetarian means?"

A little boy raised his hand, and Lily called on him.

"It means a food that isn't meat!" the boy said.

"Right!" Lily said. "Now, I love beef tacos. And chicken tacos. And salmon tacos. But today we'll make vegetarian tacos with delicious black beans, cheese, salsa, lettuce and tomatoes!"

"Yay!" a few of the more exuberant kids shouted.

"Okay, kids!" Lily began. "I've already cut up the tomatoes because using knives can be really dangerous and only adults should use sharp knives. But I want each of you to come up to my table and point out a tomato from my bowl of whole vegetables. I'll give you a hint what a tomato looks like. It's red. And round."

"I see it!" a girl shouted.

Six pairs of little legs went running over to Lily's

table, each pointing at a plump tomato in Lily's big bowl
and then taking a small bowl of cut tomatoes.

"Okay, now you can go back to your seats," Lily said.
She explained where tomatoes came from, and that they
were actually considered a fruit *and* a vegetable. There
were lots of animated questions about vines and seeds,
and then Lily asked each student to take their big measuring cup and scoop out a half cup of the cut-up tomatoes. Lily demonstrated where to find the markers on the
cups, then instructed the adults to show them closer up.

"I love tomatoes!" Wren said, jumping up and down,
her blond pigtails flying. "I know how much a half cup
is. My daddy lets me help cook!"

"That's awesome, Wren!" Lily said.

Xander shot her a smile, and Lily's knees gave a slight
shake.

She headed over to the tables to high-five kids as they
measured out the tomatoes, trying not to look at Xander.
She kept her attention on the class, sending each student
back to her teacher's table to choose a head of lettuce,
and after a mini lesson on lettuce, the kids got to shred
theirs by hand (after washing up!) and add their half
cup of lettuce to their bowls. Lily gave a little talk on
cheese next, having the kids taste three different kinds
and learning why some cheeses complemented certain
foods. Finally it was time to heat the beans, and Lily
told them all about where beans came from. For ease of
the class, she'd opened up several cans of Goya black
beans and the kids gathered around the low table where
she had a hot plate, having each kid add a pinch of the
various spices. Then the students added diced tomatoes
and spices to a bowl for the salsa, some of which ended
up on their aprons and in their hair. Finally, it was time

to learn about taco shells, and after those were heated up, everyone was excited to build their tacos with their bowl of ingredients.

"Wow," Xander said from the first row. "I had no idea tacos were so educational. I really learned quite a bit."

"Me, too," Monica trilled. "I make the best tacos, don't I, Jasper? We should invite Xander and Wren over to have them this week."

"Wren's a *girl*!" Jasper said very earnestly.

"Boys can be friends with girls, you know!" Wren shouted over her shoulder.

"Well, in any case," Monica said, "we'd love to have you over. Tuesday night?"

Was this woman really asking Xander out right here, in a children's cooking class, in front of everyone? Including his six-year-old niece? Good God.

"I appreciate the invitation," Xander told her, his voice awkward to Lily's ears, "but I'm afraid my schedule is crazy the next few months."

At least he hadn't said yes. But still!

"Ah, well, if you find yourself with a free night, just look me up. Monica Natowsky."

He gave her a tight smile and turned his attention to the taco shell that Wren was filling with her bounty.

"I can't wait to eat this!" Wren said. "Can I take a bite?" she asked Lily.

"Let's wait till everyone's tacos are assembled, because that would be extra polite, right?" Lily said.

"Right!" Wren said, looking around.

"Okay! Looks like everyone is ready. Bite!" Lily said.

The crunching was music to her ears. There was a round of *mmm*s and *this is so good* and a few *I love this class*es.

And then after cleanup and a quick Q&A, Lily dismissed the class, already missing them as the adorable little students left. Monica and Layla were among the last to leave, wistfully looking at Xander, who was deep in conversation with one of the dads.

"Uncle Xander, can I go play in the playground with Molly?" Wren asked.

"I'll watch them," the girl's dad said.

Xander smiled. "Sure, go ahead. I'll be there in a few minutes. I'm just going to say thank you to Ms. Hunt."

Wren wrapped her arms around Lily's hips, surprising her quite happily, then ran out with her friend, Molly's dad right behind them.

And now suddenly it was just Lily and Xander.

"I meant it—I had a blast," he said. "You have a real gift for teaching kids."

"Thanks. That means a lot to me. I really love working with children of all ages."

"Did you know you had a tiny fleck of cheese on your cheek?" he asked, stepping closer and reaching out his hand.

"No, actually," she whispered, her belly tightening. "I did not."

He dusted off the cheese, his brown eyes on hers, serious, intense. And unless she was delusional, which she might be, there was desire in those depths.

He leaned in.

And dammit, even if he'd discovered a black bean in her hair and was leaning close to flick that off, she was leaning in, too.

But this time, he kissed her. His hands were on her face, drawing her closer, his lips firm and soft and tender and passionate all at the same time.

Oh, my.

Yessssss!

Kissing Xander was everything she'd fantasized about—day and night—since their date in Rust Creek Falls Park.

He opened his eyes and stepped back, looking at her, his expression changing. She still saw that unexpected desire, but something else seemed to be shoving its way in. She had the feeling the kiss had taken him by surprise. That he wasn't even sure he'd meant to do it.

Nooo! Desire good. Confusion not good.

"That was some kiss," she whispered, because that was the only voice she had at the moment. "I liked it. A lot."

Sarah would be proud. So would Lily's mother. *State your intent. Stake your claim. Put yourself out there!*

There would be no take-backsies here. Not of that kiss, which she still felt burning her lips.

His smile was warm as he reached out his hand and touched her cheek. The way a man did when he cared about a woman he had just kissed passionately.

Yesss!

"I need to be honest, Lily."

Oh, cripes, she thought, her heart plummeting. *No, don't be!*

"I don't know what the hell I'm doing," he said, taking a step back and leaning against the table. "There seems to be something between us, but as I've said, I'm not looking for a relationship. I'm not looking to start something."

Jeez. Did he have to be *that* honest? Of course she wanted the truth, hard as it was to hear, but couldn't he leave her a little room to hope?

"I got burned bad right before I left Dallas," he said, running a hand through his dark hair. "I went to my girlfriend's condo to surprise her with an engagement ring, to tell her I'd stay in Texas for her instead of moving to Montana with my family. I found her in bed with my best friend—a lifelong buddy I *thought* was my best friend. I told them both to go to hell. A few days later, I left the state with my family, so that helped, but the burn... That followed me, Lily."

She reached out a hand to his arm. "I understand." Her heart ached for him, for how painful that must have been. The shock and betrayal. The loss of two people who'd meant a lot to him. Suddenly, his push-and-pull made sense.

He stared at her for a minute and it seemed like he almost wished she'd been less compassionate. As in maybe he was hoping she'd say: *Well, then don't go around kissing women you don't intend to start something with,* so that he could argue and she could huff away. Giving *him* the out.

She wouldn't ever say that. Granted, she had very little experience when it came to romance and love, but she knew how even a minor rejection had hurt. She could only imagine how hurt Xander had been and the number it had done on his head—and heart. He felt something for her, but he didn't want to *go there*.

"Well," he said, taking another step back. "I'd better go check on Wren."

She wanted him to stay, for them to keep talking—openly and honestly. But she could tell he needed some space, and his niece was waiting for him outside. "Tell her she gets an A-plus for today."

But not you, because you're keeping me at arm's length and you've got long arms.

He hurried out, the door closing behind him.

Lily touched her mouth, the feel of his lips still lingering. Now what? He'd kissed her. A real kiss. Then told her he wasn't interested in more.

Listen when someone tells you something! That would be the wise thing. But her heart was in full control of her right now, and it wanted Xander Crawford.

And Lily Hunt had never been one to *not* go for what she wanted.

After dropping Wren off with Sarah and Logan for the rest of the afternoon, Xander headed to the cattle barn. He needed to do some hard labor, some serious mucking, to get his mind unstuck. Right now, his brain was on a loop about how good it had felt to finally kiss Lily, to do what he'd been thinking about for weeks now. But then his head had come to a hard stop as if it had hit the brakes itself. He didn't know what he thought. Felt. Wanted.

He pulled on plastic gloves and grabbed a rake and headed into the back stalls. A few minutes in, he knew he was right to take on this chore instead of an afternoon off as had been the plan. His mind was already clearing.

Now all he could think about was how young Lily was. Just starting out in life. And he felt so world-weary and cynical. His trust level was nil. And that diamond ring he'd bought back in Dallas? He'd marched right back to the jeweler, needing that black velvet box out of his hands and life immediately, and thankfully, the shop had taken it back, refunding every pricey cent. That had felt good, at least. But if anyone had ever told Xander that one day he'd fall in love and plan a surprise engagement, only to end up returning the ring the next morning, he would have said they were nuts.

He heard footsteps and the humming of a Frank Sinatra song, which meant it was his dad who'd entered the barn.

Xander poked his head out of the stall to find Max Crawford pulling on a pair of black heavy-duty plastic gloves like Xander had on and then grabbing a rake, too.

"Hey, thought you had the day off," Max said. "I'm on mucking duty today."

"I know, but I could use some hard labor, so here I am."

"Fine with me," Max said. "My least favorite job on the chore chart." He and his rake went into the next stall, the strains of "Fly Me to the Moon" drifting in the air. "Interesting that you need to muck out stalls after taking Lily's cooking class. Almost like that woman has you all topsy-turvy."

He sighed and rested his chin on the top of the rake. "I guess she does. I didn't move to Montana looking for a relationship, Dad. The opposite, in fact."

"I know you had a bad breakup in Dallas, Xander. But that shouldn't hold you back from finding happiness again."

"You haven't," he said, then wished he could take it back.

But he couldn't; it was out there, hanging over the edges of their side-by-side stalls.

Hell, maybe it was good to finally have this conversation. His dad hadn't remarried, hadn't gotten serious with a woman Xander's entire life.

Because his wife walking out on him, on their family, had been unbearable.

"Sorry," Xander said, feeling like a heel. "That's your business and I have no right—"

"Yes, you do," Max said. "You have every right. If I'm going to push a determined wedding planner on you and your brothers, you have a right to know why I don't practice what I preach."

Xander came out of the stall and stood in the doorway of his dad's. His father was tall and imposing but somehow looked so...vulnerable.

"I just want you boys to be happy. To have what I didn't. I might have given up on happiness for myself but hell if I'm gonna stand by and watch what that taught you boys. You need love. Partners. Family. That's what makes the world go round, Xan. Bitterness just makes it come to a screeching halt."

Xander nodded, and then walked into the stall and embraced his dad, Max stiffening with clear surprise at first, and then hugging him back. "I know. Believe me."

He headed back into his stall and started mucking away. And for the next couple of hours, he and his dad worked in silence, Xander's mind clearer but no answers on the horizon.

Chapter Seven

Communication from Xander Crawford following The Kiss:

Sunday night, a text: Thanks again for the fun and informative cooking class today. Wren had a great time.

Response: My pleasure.

Monday morning: I woke up craving lobster rolls for some reason. On the specials menu at MM?

Response: No, sorry.

Monday night: Lobster rolls tomorrow?

Response: No, sorry.

Later Monday night: Jeez, I thought I had an in with the chef.

No response.

Tuesday morning: Just checking in.

Response: Smiley face emoji. Super busy—have a great day!

The old Lily might have raced over to Kalispell Monday morning to buy lobster and all the fixings for lobster rolls. Eager to please. Like a puppy. The old Lily might also have kept the text conversation going on Tuesday by asking open-ended questions.

But a new Lily had taken root inside her—every day, with every satisfied diner at the Maverick Manor, every "great job, Lily" from her boss, every decent grade on her schoolwork, every time she understood a difficult business concept. Add to it these new feelings for a man—the first time she'd truly fallen in love—and Lily felt different in her bones. Like a woman instead of a kid.

On Wednesday afternoon, Lily bit into her cruller at Daisy's Donuts, Sarah Crawford sipping her iced latte while baby Sophia napped in her stroller at their table by the window. She filled in Sarah on the big kiss and the conversation that followed—not the details of what Xander had shared about his ex, but just the gist that he had a big closed sign over his heart.

Sarah's eyes lit up. "This kiss says everything!"

"I want to hope so. But he told me he's not looking to start anything. *That* actually says everything."

"He's a cowboy who's been kicked in the head by unexpected love," Sarah said. "He needs time to reclaim his own mind. And when he does, watch out, Lily."

Lily laughed. "I love your optimism. But I won't hold my breath." She bit her lip, thinking about that kiss. Sometimes she could still feel the imprint of his lips. "You know what? I'm not even going to think about it. Xander needs to figure out how he feels, right? I think I should just take a step back. Kind of like I was doing with my responses to his texts."

Sarah took a bite of her chocolate cider donut. "I have

to say that the way you responded to those messages sure kept them coming. I love the 'Just checking in.'" She laughed. "Poor guy."

Lily smiled. "I like this newer, wiser me. I'm not sitting around endlessly thinking about him and his deal. I'm focusing on work, school and my future. Which I hope includes him, of course," she admitted.

"I have faith," Sarah said with a big nod.

Lily sipped her own iced latte and couldn't help but notice again how nice Sarah looked—for just coffee out with a friend. Sarah wore pale pink capri pants, a white tank top with a ruffled hem around the V-neck, and adorable multicolored leather sandals that wrapped around her ankles three times. She was the sleep-deprived mother of a baby and yet she wore a little makeup and earrings and she smelled like a hint of perfume—not baby spit-up. She looked this way because she wanted to. It truly had to be that simple.

"I want a makeover," Lily said.

Sarah's eyes lit up. "Ooh!"

"I want to look like *me*—the me I've never explored because I was too busy wanting to fit in with my brothers and be accepted by them. I want my outside to match all the changes I've made on the inside. I'm going for my dreams."

"Including the six-foot-two-inch one?" her friend asked.

Lily smiled, then bit her lip. "Crazy thing is, Sarah—he likes me *this* way. Salsa on my cheek, onion-scented hands, loose jeans, no makeup, no style. He likes me as I am." The truth of it practically knocked the breath out of her. The way he looked at her—even on that first non-date in the park—was proof. The kiss was proof.

Xander Crawford likes me, she thought, a rush of happiness swelling in her belly. *He's attracted to* me.

"Okay, now I'm going to cry," Sarah said, tearing up. "I know exactly what you mean."

"But wanting this makeover is for *me*. About *me*. I want to find out who I am if I let myself really go for it. So will you help me?"

"Is right now too soon?" Sarah asked with a grin. "I wish I didn't have my dentist appointment in fifteen minutes or we could take off for Kalispell now and hit the shops and salon."

"Need me to babysit?" Lily asked.

"Actually, I have a sitter all lined up who should arrive any minute now."

"Oh, well next time, call me," Lily said. "I love taking care of Sophia." She looked at the beautiful sleeping baby, her bow lips quirking.

One day, I want a Sophia of my own, she thought— for the first time. She sucked in a breath as a sense of absolute wonder overtook her. She'd never really thought about getting married or having children; she'd always figured she would, but the notion had always seemed a few years down the road. Several years.

Lily bit her lip again as she wondered if falling in love with Xander Crawford had anything to do with her sudden baby fever.

"How about tomorrow morning for the makeover?" Sarah asked. "Ooh, Lily—you can debut your new look at the dance Saturday night!"

"I wasn't planning on going," she said, thinking about the Rust Creek Falls Summer Sunset Dance, held every year in a different location. The whole town always turned up, apparently—well, except her, and no one had ever asked her to the dance, not that she couldn't have gone with a girlfriend. Dances had never been her thing. Starting with semiformals in middle school and working up to the senior prom, which she hadn't gone to, either.

"I know for a fact Xander will be there," Sarah said, wriggling her eyebrows. "All the Crawfords are going."

"Oh, great," Lily said. "I can watch Xander dance with every single beauty in town. Wonderful way to pass the time."

"Want to know a secret?" Sarah asked. "But you can't tell Xander I told you."

Lily leaned closer. "Scout's honor." She held up three fingers.

"Logan confided in me that Xander actually told Viv Dalton to only set him up with women he'd have nothing in common with. Viv reported him to Max, their dad, who was asking for a status report and why Xander wasn't engaged yet." Sarah laughed. "That man. Seriously."

"Nothing in common with?" Lily repeated. "Why bother, then?"

"Want to know Logan's theory?"

Lily leaned closer again.

"Logan thinks his brother is trying to just get his dad off his back—by dating at all—and only agreeing to dates with women he won't fall for because he's already fallen for someone and can't deal."

Lily's eyes widened. "That's some theory."

"With a lot of truth to it. Doesn't that sound about right?"

"I'm hardly used to flattering myself, Sarah. The man kissed me. Once. That doesn't mean anything."

"We'll see," Sarah said with a devious grin. "So tomorrow—girlie day in Kalispell?"

"I have to be at work at four. Otherwise I'm free."

Sarah actually clapped with excitement. "Can't wait."

Huh. The *new* new Lily at the Summer Sunset Dance. With Xander in attendance. Could be very interesting.

"There's my adorable niece," came a very familiar masculine voice.

"Did I mention my sitter is Xander and that I asked him to meet me here?" Sarah asked with yet another devilish grin as she stood up. "How nice that both of you are in the same place at the same time and will have to communicate in person. You might even ask him to the dance Saturday night," she whispered.

Ooh, Sarah was good—Lily had to hand it to her. Even if she wanted to bop her friend over the head with the rest of her cruller.

Sarah then leaned over the stroller to give Sophia a kiss on the forehead. "Be good for Uncle Xander and Auntie Lily," she whispered.

Lily's eyes widened. Auntie Lily. Uncle Xander.

Technically, Lily had always been Auntie Lily, before Sarah had even married into the Crawford family.

"Xander, thank you so much for babysitting!" Sarah said. "Lucky for me I ran into you at the Ambling A this morning just when I was fretting over needing care at the last minute. Turns out I could have asked Lily since she has the afternoon off."

Yup, Sarah was *good*.

He smiled, giving Lily a nod but keeping his attention on Sarah. "My pleasure, really. Least I can do since you'll be stuck in a dentist's chair." He turned to Lily. "Nice to see you," he said awkwardly.

"You, too," she said.

Sarah gave her a quick hug, gave Xander a quick rundown on what to expect—which was Sophia sleeping for the next hour—thanked him again and then dashed out.

"So you're free right now?" Xander said. "Want to help me babysit? I'd do anything for my sister-in-law, but if Sophia wakes up, I have no idea what to do. Logan gave me a few lessons over the past few months in how to hold her, but I'm not even good at *that*."

Lily laughed. "Consider me at your service."

He blushed slightly, and maybe she shouldn't have said that. Of course, she hadn't meant anything flirty by it, but hell, she was the new her and maybe she *had*.

Xander tried not to stare at Lily, but he could barely drag his eyes off her. The past few days he'd thought of little else besides that incredible kiss in the rec center kitchen. And he needed to concentrate when he was working at the Ambling A. Yesterday he'd almost knocked himself out by stepping on a rake he hadn't noticed lying across the barn floor. This morning, his brother Finn had apparently said "Earth to Xander" three times before he realized someone was asking him something out by a pasture fence.

So when he'd run into Sarah, who'd looked frantic about a dentist appointment and needing someone to watch Sophia, he'd volunteered. Babies slept a lot, right? He figured he'd park his keister in Daisy's for the hour and a half, drink three or four caffeinated beverages, give the stroller a gentle rock if Sophia got fussy, and have a little time to himself to get his head clear.

He was having to do that a lot lately.

And here, right in front of him, was the woman keeping his head in the clouds.

A little wail came from the stroller, a tiny fist jutting out in complaint.

"Someone woke up on the wrong side of the stroller this afternoon," Xander said with a smile. He unbuckled the harness and carefully scooped out Sophia, holding her the way Logan had taught him and rubbing her back. Hey, this was as easy as he thought it would be.

Until Sophia started screeching.

"Thought I was getting the knack of this," Xander said, frowning. "Guess not."

Sophia's cheeks were red and she started waving her tiny fists.

"It's me. Uncle Xan," he said, rocking her side to side and bouncing her in his arms. "Peekaboo!"

"Waaah!" Sophia screamed.

"What am I doing wrong?" Xander asked.

"Sometimes a baby just gets fussy and needs a new face," Lily said. "Want me to try?"

"Waah!"

"Please," he said, handing Sophia over.

Lily took the baby, rubbing her back and cooing to her. Sophia seemed to like that. She was still flailing her arms but her cheeks were less red. "There, there," she whispered, rubbing her back some more.

Sophia stopped crying.

"Lucky you were here. Or Eva would have kicked me and Sophia out," he said, sending a rueful smile over to the donut shop manager behind the counter.

"How'd you get so good with babies?" Xander asked. "You're the baby of your family."

"I've always babysat. Since I was twelve. And before I started offering cooking classes to supplement my income, I worked part-time at a day care in the infant room."

"I've done group-brother babysitting so that Logan and Sarah could get some time to themselves, and among the five of us, we did pretty well, thanks to Hunter, who knows what he's doing. I thought I had this."

Lily laughed. "I can just picture you Crawford brothers hovering around a tiny baby, trying to figure her out."

"We're pretty clueless, but hey, we do love our niece."

"She's one lucky little girl to have such doting uncles." She gazed at Sophia, giving her another bounce and letting her stretch her legs. The baby seemed much happier. "Well, I've got the next couple hours free, so I'm happy to help. Why don't we head to my house and change her and give her a bottle if she's hungry, then take her for a walk?"

He liked the idea on two counts. He'd have a pro with him just in case and he'd get to spend time with Lily. "Sounds good. And thanks."

Sophia did not want to go back in the stroller, so Lily held her while Xander wheeled the stroller out of Daisy's Donuts.

"Hi, Xander!" trilled a feminine voice.

Lily glanced up to see a pretty woman with long dark hair and an amazing body smiling at Xander as she approached the shop. The brunette gave Lily a quick assessing glance, seemingly decided she was no competition and turned her megawatt smile back to the hot rancher.

Xander nodded politely and kept walking, the woman's sexy smile turning into a sulky frown.

"Get that a lot, huh?" she asked as they headed up North Broomtail Road.

Who'd think it would be such a drag to have attractive women throwing themselves at you? But it was.

"Thanks to my dad, yes," he said. "First there are the women who are looking to meet Mr. Right, and my dad created his own dating service with six men. Now five. Then there are the women who heard a rumor that my dad promised Viv Dalton a million bucks to get us all married, and they figure there's big money in the family. So, double whammy."

Lily smiled. "Don't forget the women who simply like the idea of going on a date with an interesting cowboy newcomer. That was me, you know. When Viv asked if I wanted to be set up with Knox, I wasn't thinking about marriage or a million dollars. I was just thinking it sounded like fun. A rancher from Texas? With five brothers? I'd bet we'd have a lot to talk about."

"Touché," he said. "But women like you are few and far between."

"I don't know about that, Xander. I think women and men—everyone—just want what their heart desires."

"That's a nice way of putting it," he said.

"People are just people, Xander. Not everyone is for everyone—that's the thing to know. Everything else is none of our business."

"Meaning?"

"Let's use your family as an example. Knox clearly wasn't the guy for me. If he was, he'd have gone on the date. But he didn't so we didn't get the opportunity to see if there was something there. You stepped in, and we hit it off. Knox and his reasons for canceling are not my concern or my business. What matters is who I *do* connect with. Not who I don't and the reasons why."

"You learned this in Economics 101?" he asked.

Lily laughed. "I've been doing a lot of thinking lately about what draws people together and pulls them apart. Why some people work and some don't. Half is chemistry and half is timing."

"I'll buy that. And if the timing is wrong?"

"Then that chemistry goes to waste. All that connection, interest, fun, desire, sharing, talking, laughing—buh-bye."

He glanced at her. "That seems like a shame."

"Yup, sure does."

For a twenty-three-year-old newbie at life, she sure was smart about human interaction, he thought. Maybe too smart.

They arrived at Lily's house, Sophia still content and surveying the world—or Rust Creek Falls—from Lily's arms. As they headed in, Xander hoped he'd run into Andrew so he could find out how things were going with Heidi. The two had gone out a bunch of times already. And they were a good example of what Lily was talking about. Xander hadn't been the guy for Heidi, but one suggestion of Andrew Hunt and voilà—they were practically engaged.

Chemistry and timing. If you had both, you had everything.

He and Lily had chemistry, but the timing? Not so good.

The Hunt house turned out be empty. Everyone was still at work, so Lily suggested they hang out in the living room and let Sophia crawl around the big soft rug. But first, Lily took her in the bathroom to change her, and strange as it was, he missed the two of them when they were gone, even for the two minutes it took Lily to return with a smiling Sophia in her arms.

They both lay down on opposite sides of the rug to create a pen of sorts for Sophia, making peekaboo faces to get her to crawl to them. Sophia shrieked with delight every time Xander revealed his face. He laughed, having too good a time playing house with Lily and Sophia.

Way too good a time.

As Sophia crawled all over Lily, the beautiful redhead making exaggerated faces at the baby and blowing raspberries on her belly, he was completely transfixed.

He could see himself coming home to Lily and their baby.

Whoa, he thought, bolting upright. Where had *that* come from?

"So how many kids do you want?" Lily asked. "Someday, I mean."

"Honestly, I've never really thought about that. I like the idea of a big family like I had, older siblings, younger siblings. Always someone around."

"I don't know about the younger siblings, but I liked growing up in a big family, too. I always envisioned four kids at least."

"Four little redheads," he said with a grin. "And freckles across their noses."

She touched a hand to her nose. "These were the bane of my existence when I was a teenager. I've gotten used to them."

"I like freckles." *I like* your *freckles. I like everything about you.*

The smile that lit up her face almost did him in. He watched her lift Sophia into her arms and hoist her high in the air. *Focus on the baby, not the woman. You're babysitting. That's all that's going on here.*

His father had set some crazy roller coaster on high

speed and so, Xander had met Lily Hunt in the first place. Otherwise, he wouldn't know her. He'd be working the Ambling A, focusing on renovating the ranch, his new family home—his new life. Falling for a woman who could destroy him with a snap of her fingers? No, thank you. Not again. He might have feelings for Lily, but hell if he'd let them go deeper than he already had.

To reinforce that, he let himself think about something he'd forced from his mind six weeks ago.

Britney in bed with Chase. The woman he'd been about to propose to. And his lifelong best friend.

We're so sorry. We didn't mean for it to happen. We're in love, Xander. This isn't just some affair.

Yeah, that made it better.

He felt himself tightening up, the walls closing in. Good. Because he felt like himself again. Like the man he'd been the past six weeks. Keeping to himself. Working hard.

Ping.

The sound shook him out of his bad memories, and he leaned his head back, sucking in a breath.

Lily had received a text, and as Sophia crawled over to him, Lily grabbed her phone. "Sarah's all done." Lily texted something back. "She'll be by to pick up Sophia in a few minutes."

Good. He needed to get out of here. Breathe some open air.

Relief flooded him when Sarah arrived. Lily settled the baby back in her stroller, and there it was again, that tug of his heart as he watched her. He was barely aware of the small talk he made about what a good baby Sophia was, how Lily had saved the day with her mad baby skills. The door closed behind Sarah, and then it was just the two of them.

Leave. Head to the door. Go.

But he was rooted to the floor. He wanted out. He wanted to stay. He didn't know what the hell he wanted.

"Thanks for helping out," he said. Awkwardly, with his hands in his pockets. "I guess I'll go now."

"Any time," she said.

And still he didn't move.

They stared at each other for a moment, both just... standing there.

"You know, you never did get your cooking lesson, Xander. If you have time now, I could show you how to make a delicious bacon and cheese omelet, which is exactly what I'm craving this second."

You should leave. This woman has mystical, magical powers over you.

Which was clearly why he *couldn't* leave. And besides, he was hungry.

"That does sound really good." He followed her into the kitchen, dying to pull her into his arms and kiss her again.

But she now had a carton of eggs in her hands, and had instructed him to crack five in a bowl. He was so focused on her face, her freckles, her lips that he hadn't heard half of what she'd said in the past few minutes.

He took the carton and got busy cracking, getting only two little bits of shell in, which Lily scooped out with a spoon.

"Anyone home?" a male voice shouted from the front door.

Good thing, too. Because he'd been about to lean in

again. Close. Despite everything he'd been feeling just ten minutes ago.

"Sounds like Andrew," Lily said. "In the kitchen," she called back.

"What else is new?" Andrew said as he came sauntering in with Heidi right behind him. He smiled. "Ah, *this* is new," he said at the sight of Xander. "Or is it?" he asked with a grin.

"Xander and I are friends," Lily said, cutting her flashing green eyes at her brother.

"Got it," Andrew repeated with a little too much mirth in his voice. "You're just friends."

"Xander," Heidi said with a warm smile, "did I ever thank you for fixing me up with Andrew? I've meant to."

"I'm glad it worked out," Xander said.

"It's worked out and then some," Andrew said, dipping Heidi and giving her a dramatic kiss.

Heidi laughed and swatted him. "I'll tell ya," she said to Xander and Lily, "over the past few months I must have gone on thirty dates. I thought maybe I was just too picky or that I'd never find my guy. And then out of nowhere, a date very strangely fixes me up with another date—and he's the one. You just never know. Life is crazy."

"I love that," Lily said. "And I agree. You just never know. Being open, saying yes—that's how you find what you really need."

"Exactly," Heidi said.

Again, he thought about what Lily had said about chemistry and timing. Heidi could have so easily told him no way, that she didn't need a blah date setting her up with her next blah date. But she'd been open to possibilities, and now it looked like she and Andrew were headed somewhere serious.

Possibilities. Exactly what he didn't want to explore. For damned good reasons.

"So I'm giving Xander a cooking lesson on the art of omelets," Lily told her brother and Heidi. "Bacon and cheese. If you guys are hungry, stick around and you could join us."

"I love bacon," Andrew said. "So I guess this is our first double date, Lily."

"Just *friends*, remember?" Lily said.

Did "just friends" want to kiss her the way he'd imagined doing a second ago? No.

"I'm going to try not to burn the bacon," Xander said to change the subject. He grabbed the package from the counter and used a knife to slit open the side.

"Well, we'll be in the living room," Andrew said. "Sorry in advance about all the PDA you might be forced to witness."

He got another swat from Heidi for that, and then Xander was once again alone with Lily in the kitchen.

"They're very sweet," Lily said. "I'm so happy for my brother. His life is really coming together. Now if you could just get Bobby and Ryan hooked up, they'll be out of my hair, too."

He laughed. "Sorry, but I told Viv I'm done with the fix-ups. So I won't have any referrals to make."

She stared at him. "Oh?"

He nodded, using the tongs to lay the bacon in the big square fry pan. *I thought I could stop thinking about you by dating women I'd never really be interested in. But nothing makes me stop thinking about you.*

Silencing that inner voice, he barked at himself, *Get*

*your mind back on the cooking lesson. Get control of
your own head, man.*

"So you were saying I can pan-fry bacon or bake it
in the oven?" he asked. "I think my dad bakes it. Half
the time it's burned."

"That might be a temperature issue. And keeping it
in too long. With bacon, you have to keep a steady eye.
I like frying because the smell fills the air faster and I
like how the oil jumps in the pan. I know, I'm crazy."

He smiled. "It's fun getting your wrist singed by splat-
ters of burning oil?".

She laughed. "I've been through it all, cooking wise.
I can take a little heat."

*Can you? You're twenty-three. So young. So innocent.
So...idealistic.*

Her idealism was one of the reasons he admired her
so much.

God, he wanted to kiss her.

She started talking about cooking temperatures, but
he missed everything she said. Her long red hair, despite
being pulled back into a ponytail, made him want to run
his hands through it. He wanted to kiss every freckle
dotting her nose and cheeks.

"Smells good!" Andrew called from the living room.

Xander had barely been aware the bacon was frying.
He made himself pay attention as she showed him how
to scramble the eggs, which of course he knew, how to
let the omelet set and cook at the same time, when to
add the cheese and bacon and when to fold it. They had
two pans going, two omelets in each, and suddenly they
were ready and smelled amazing. The ones he was responsible for looked a little lopsided, but still delicious.

"We'll eat these," he said. "My first diners can have yours."

She laughed, and again he wanted to pull her against him and just hug her, hold her.

He didn't know how long he was going to be able to contain his feelings for her. If he even should at this point. Maybe they could just see what was between them. Maybe it wouldn't last, they could get each other out of their system, and he could go back to being Not Getting Involved Xander.

"Going to the dance at Sunshine Farm on Saturday night?" he asked as she showed him how to slide the omelet onto a plate.

He suddenly imagined them pressed chest to chest, her arms draped around his neck, his around her waist as they swayed to a slow country ballad. The warm, breezy summer air blowing back her long red hair...

She added a handful of grapes to each plate. "I was just talking to Sarah about it today. The Rust Creek Falls Summer Sunset Dance. Sounds fun. Will you be there?"

"I think all the Crawfords are going, so yes. I'll show my face but I don't know how long I'll stay."

"Well, I'll definitely see you there, then. You'll save me a dance before you rush off into the night?"

"I will," he said, dragging his eyes off her and onto the plates.

It was almost like a date. But not quite. He'd see how it felt, dancing with Lily. Thinking of her as his. A slow ease into giving in to his feelings for her.

It was a start, right?

Chapter Eight

Kalispell was the nearest big town to Rust Creek Falls, a forty-five minute drive but worth it for the access to shops where Lily could look through clothing racks and jewelry displays, and maybe even get her makeup done at a beauty counter. She'd been going to Bee's Beauty Parlor, which was right next door to two of her favorite places—Daisy's Donuts and Wings to Go—ever since her dad realized her hair would need trimming every few months and that his attempts were woefully uneven. Lily had even called Bee's to make an appointment for a real haircut, but they were booked solid because of the dance. Luckily Sarah had gotten recommendations for salons in Kalispell and now Lily was sitting in a huge swivel chair in Hair Genie, a trendy-looking salon in the center of town, Sarah standing beside her.

"So what do you have in mind?" her stylist, Ember

(Lily had no idea if that was her real name or not), a chic young woman all in black, asked as she assessed Lily's hair, running her fingers through it, picking up strands and examining the ends. "Very healthy. You can do anything with this thick, straight, silky texture."

Lily looked at Ember's gorgeous mane, which was exactly what she wanted hers to look like. "I love *your* hairstyle. Would that work on me?"

Ember smiled and nodded. "Absolutely. I just have some simple long layers. Keeps it easy for me to pin up so it doesn't get in my way when I'm working, but the layers give the thick, straight texture a lot of oomph and swing."

"That's perfect for you, Lily," Sarah said, standing on the other side of her and looking at her reflection. "Lily's a chef," she told Ember.

"Then it's vital to keep the front layers very long so they don't fall in your face," Ember said. "Plus, you can dress up the cut or keep it casual—just like with fashion. Let it air-dry or a quick blow-dry for a casual look. Use a heated styling brush or curling iron and you can do amazing beachy waves."

"Perfect. I put myself in your hands," she told Ember. Then she grinned at Sarah. "I'm so excited!"

"Me, too," Sarah said. "Okay, I'm gonna go read magazines—something I never get to do."

Lily looked at the shiny silver scissors in Ember's hand and felt like this moment marked the culmination of everything she'd worked so hard for the past year. Working toward her degree in business. Quitting the Gold Rush Diner for a swanky restaurant like the Maverick Manor and getting promoted to line cook (she had been a prep cook her first six months, but the few times she'd filled in for a cook had caught her boss's attention). Making plans, even if they were just in her head at this point, for having her own place someday, whether a small restaurant or her own catering shop or even both. Her look would now catch up with the woman she'd become on the inside.

She closed her eyes, wanting her haircut to be a surprise.

Twenty-five minutes later, Ember announced she was all done and that it was time to unveil the new Lily Hunt. Sarah came running over and Lily heard her gasp.

She opened her eyes.

Wow. "I love it!" Lily shrieked. Her hair was still long, the layers starting at her shoulders and flipping back a bit to blend in with the rest of her hair. Ember had her move her head from side to side like she was in a shampoo commercial.

"You look amazing!" Sarah said. "It's gorgeous! Chic and stylish but still casual at the same time. It's perfect!"

Lily shot out of her chair and threw her arms around Ember.

The stylist laughed. "I love getting that reaction. See you in six weeks for a trim. Or since you live a bit of a distance, you can just have a local salon keep up the trims, and come to me if you want to make another change. I am your hair genie," she added with a grin and bow.

"Squee!" Lily shouted as she and Sarah left the salon. She couldn't stop touching her hair and shaking it. "I'm going to make you sick after a while, Sarah."

"I completely get your excitement," her friend said. "Ooh, let's check out that clothing shop." She pointed across the street at On Trend, a boutique. "Look at that pretty dress in the window."

Lily was already staring at it. It was a knee-length sundress, a pale pink with spaghetti straps. Sexy and playful. And perfect for the dance.

They linked arms and dashed across the street and into the shop.

Lily found the dress in her size and slung it over her arm, then Sarah directed her to the racks of jeans, wagging her finger when Lily looked at a pair of her usual type of jeans.

"Try these," Sarah said, picking up a pair of dark-wash skinny jeans. "And these. And these."

A saleswoman gathered what they'd chosen so far and hung the items in a dressing room. Sarah came over with armloads of tops and sweaters and pants. Lily had an armful of her own.

Ten minutes later, Lily was in the dressing room. She started with the pale pink dress.

She took off her T-shirt and shorts and slid the dress over her head, the soft fabric lovely against her skin. It fit perfectly, neither tight nor loose. She stood back and looked at herself, tears poking her eyes.

Yes. Yes, yes, yes. This is me.

She stepped out of the dressing room and Sarah literally clapped.

"It's beautiful! It fits you so well! Oh, Lily!"

Lily stared at herself in the floor mirror. "I always shied away from pinks because of my hair, but something about the light pink works. Have I ever worn spaghetti straps? I don't think so."

"You look amazing," Sarah said.

"Want to try these cute shoes with it?" the salesclerk

asked, holding out a pair of silver ballet flats with a pointy toe.

The shoes looked great with the dress and were shockingly comfortable for not being sneakers or the clogs Lily usually wore to work.

A half hour later, Lily brought her "yes" pile to the counter, her gaze drawn to the intimates section. "Maybe a couple of sexy bras and matching undies would round out the plain white cotton and little purple flowers on my current collection."

"Definitely," Sarah said with a grin.

Two lace bras, one a blush color, one black, and two matching pairs of underwear joined the stack on the counter. She was getting the dress, two pairs of skinny jeans, two pairs of slim capris, one black pencil skirt, three tops with cute details and two pretty cardigans. Plus three pairs of shoes—the silver ballet flats, a pair of charcoal leather heels that she could actually walk in and strappy sandals. All the pieces worked together so that she'd have outfits. She couldn't wait to move her current wardrobe of loose, boring jeans and T-shirts to the back of her closet.

Next they stopped in a cosmetics shop, a saleswoman giving her a tutorial on a natural and an evening look. When the woman capped the pink-red lipstick and Lily looked in the mirror at her makeover, she gasped again.

"Whoa. I've never worn this much makeup. But it doesn't look like I'm playing dress-up. It just looks like an enhanced me."

"Exactly," the woman said. "You look very elegant."

"Me, elegant," Lily repeated. "First time anyone's ever called me that!"

Sarah grinned. "Welcome, Enhanced Lily!"

Lily laughed, peering at herself in the mirror, still unable to believe she could look like this if she wanted. "I wonder if Xander will even notice."

Sarah's eyes probably popped. "What? Are you serious?"

Lily sighed. "I don't think what I look like is the issue."

"Well, if the T-shirt and jeans Lily has that man all wrung inside out," Sarah said, "imagine what the sexy Lily is gonna do to him!"

Huh. She hadn't thought of it like that before.

Lily grinned.

"Yes, you're going," Max Crawford bellowed at Knox in the family room at the Ambling A on Saturday afternoon. "And you're going," he said, pointing at Hunter. "And you're going." This was directed at Finn. "The kvetching around here—over a casual summer dance. Give me a break! You're all going and that's that!"

"Well, I guess we're going," Wilder said on a chuckle.

"No one wondered if *you* were going," Knox said to Wilder, a guy who'd always lived up his name. "Of course you're going."

"Damned straight I am," Wilder confirmed. "At least thirty women asked me to save them a dance."

Little did those women know that Wilder was about as interested in marriage as Xander was.

"Ditto," Finn said.

Now *there* was the single women of Rust Creek Falls's best chance of Viv Dalton's "dating service" ending with a walk down the aisle. The dreamer of the family, Finn was always falling in love. Out of love just as fast and hard, but then back in love—with the same enthusiasm. Xander didn't get it.

"Just thirty?" Hunter asked. "Try at least a hundred here."

"Once again," Knox said, "I doubt there are a hundred single women in this town."

"Feels like it, thanks to dear old Dad," Hunter pointed out.

Knox gave a firm nod. "That's the truth."

Logan rolled his eyes. "Oh, you poor, poor guys. Going to a social event where you'll dance with women and have some good food and meet new people."

"Oh, shut up," Xander said. "Once you settled down with Sarah, you were able to walk along the streets of this town in peace again. You have no idea what we go through." He grinned and held up a palm for a high five from Wilder, sitting next to him on the sofa.

Logan threw a pillow at him, and Xander's gaze caught on his brother's wedding ring. Xander sure hadn't seen that coming—the marriage—but Logan had surprised them all. Not only had he fallen crazy in love but with a single mother of a baby. Watching his older brother become a father to little Sophia sometimes stopped Xander in his tracks, stole his breath. Because it was so unexpected? Because it made Xander wonder about himself and whether he'd have a family of his own someday? A wife, a baby? Despite all his head-shaking to the contrary, the thought of a wife and child had been creeping into Xander's head lately.

Like at Lily's house. When they were babysitting Sophia. When he was watching Lily with his niece. All sorts of insane ideas flew through his mind.

Eh, he thought. One Crawford brother out of six did

not mean they were all headed in the direction Logan had gone. He glanced at his brother, who always looked happy these days. Content. Purposeful.

Logan had the lightest hair of the six Crawfords—that *had* to have something to do with it. The darker-haired brothers would remain single the way they were supposed to.

While Finn and Wilder got in an arm-wrestling match, Knox and Logan betting on the winner, and Hunter confirming with his sitter what time she'd be over to watch Wren, Xander took the opportunity to slip away unnoticed. He headed up to his bedroom and shut the door on the voices and laughter in the family room.

Two hours until the dance. Xander moved over to the window overlooking the front of the house, the pastures and fields, the cattle just standing there calming him down. He had no idea what he was so revved up about, anyway.

Because he thought of tonight as a date of sorts? It wouldn't be, not really. It was just a casual dance, being held outdoors at Sunshine Farm, which Eva and Luke Stockton had turned into a guest ranch last year. Sure, he'd dance with Lily once, maybe twice. He'd probably stay for a half hour and then leave.

He'd lost track of how many women asked *him* to save them a dance. Except for one. The only one that mattered. Lily. Which meant maybe he should dance with a lot of women. He might have Lily Hunt on the brain but he didn't want to.

You followed your heart once before, and you got slammed in the gut with a sharp right hook. Punched in the head, too. Knocked out. That was how it still felt.

Britney and Chase were married now. Just like that.

They'd flown to Vegas, figuring their families and friends would stop giving them a hard time about their sudden union and how they'd betrayed "that poor Xander" if they proved they were the real deal. So they'd taken a road trip and married in a chapel in some fancy hotel.

Xander knew this because Chase had written him; how he got his address in Montana, Xander had no clue. But Chase had sent a letter, a real letter, not an email, again saying he was sorry about what happened, that he'd mourn the end of their friendship for the rest of his life, but that he found the right woman, the only woman, and though it killed him that she was his best friend's woman, Britney was his life.

The letter had arrived a couple weeks after Xander had moved to Montana with his family. At the time, he'd quickly read it and almost ripped it up, but then shoved it back in the envelope and stashed it in his top dresser drawer under a pile of socks, where things went to die. Like the one photo he had of his mother. Like a photo of him, Britney and Chase at a carnival photo booth.

Xander went to his dresser and stuck his hand under a bunch of rolled socks until he found the photo. Britney, long blond hair everywhere, Chase with his military-short cut and Xander, with his long dark hair. In one of the four little black-and-white photos, Britney was laughing uproariously at something Chase said while Xander laughed, too. Now that he thought about it, their romance had probably started that day.

Interesting that Xander had held on to the photo. He had no idea why he had—and didn't want to think about it right now. Back under the socks it went, the dresser door shoved shut.

He moved over to his bed and dropped down on it, his gaze landing on his bedside table, on the old diary lying there. Xander had almost forgotten about the diary entirely. He and his brothers had been replacing the rotted floorboards in this room, which Xander had wanted because it faced the front yard and he always liked to face forward, when they found something buried. A jewel-encrusted diary with the letter *A* on the front. *A* for the Ambling A? The ranch had come with the name, and they'd all liked it, liked the unknown history that was behind it, so they'd kept it. Plus, they were ambling men themselves, weren't they?

The diary was worn with time and age—and locked. Someone had buried this diary under the floorboard and had either forgotten about it or passed away. The Ambling A had been a vacant mess for decades until the Crawfords bought the property and started renovating, so who knew how long the diary had been buried under the floor. Or why. Xander had thought about trying to pick the lock, to see if there was anything interesting in the diary about the Ambling A, ranch secrets or a clue to whose diary it was, but a simple attempt to get the lock open hadn't worked and then he just lost interest in the old journal. He wasn't one to write down his thoughts and feelings, though maybe it would help.

Dear Diary,

I found the woman I was about to propose to in bed with my best friend. People suck. Love sucks. Forget the whole damned thing.

Yup, that was how his diary would start. Then maybe he'd get to something like this:

Dear Diary,

There's a redhead named Lily who has me all be-

witched. She's not my type. At all. Except for the fact that I can't stop thinking about her or imagining myself in bed with her. So does that make her my type? I guess it does.

Xander gave a rueful chuckle and stood up. He was losing his mind.

While he was pulling out a shirt, he envisioned himself dancing with Lily under the stars, in the moonlight, his woman in his arms.

His woman? He was *definitely* losing his mind.

Chapter Nine

"What?" Andrew Hunt said on a croak.

Lily, halfway down the stairs of her house, almost took her phone out of her new little beaded cross-body purse so that she could snap a photo of her brother's face and his priceless expression. *Surprised* didn't begin to capture it as he stood in the foyer.

Or Bobby's. Or Ryan's. Or her father's.

"What?" Andrew repeated, his mouth still dropped open, jaw to the floor.

"Lily?" Ryan asked, peering closer at her as he came out of the kitchen with a beer.

"That's not Lily," Bobby, right behind Ryan, said with a firm shake of his head. "Who are you and what have you done with our baby sister?"

"Oh, my God, that is definitely Lily," her father said, one hand over his mouth, another over his heart.

Oh, brother—literally. She sucked in a breath and finished walking down the stairs, the four Hunts staring at her, mouths still agape.

"I mean, Lily, I've seen you in a dress a time or two," Andrew said, "but this isn't just you in a dress. This is..."

"Lily as a nominee at the Academy Awards," Bobby said. "Wow," he added.

"Fairy Godmother up in your room or something?" Ryan asked, the Hunt green eyes completely confused.

"Can't a girl doll up a little for a dance?" she asked innocently, moving over to the large mirror above a console table in the hallway. She checked her appearance for a stray bit of mascara or something in her teeth.

But nope—she was camera ready.

She'd gone with the pale pink sundress with the spaghetti straps, the hem ending in a swish just above her knees. She wore the pretty earrings she'd bought in Kalispell, silver filigree hoops, and three delicate silver bangles on her left arm. The ballet slippers, which kept the outfit casual and simple, were perfect for an outdoor dance at Sunshine Farm. Makeup, including the famous "smoky" eye Sarah had taught her to do, a sweep of mascara, pink-red lipstick, her layered hair all shiny, bouncy and loose, and a spritz of a perfume sample she'd gotten in the boutique—and she was all ready to go.

Oh, and the blush-colored lace bra and panties underneath it all.

She took a final glance at herself in the mirror, gave her hair a fluff and turned toward the Hunts, who were still all staring at her.

"Uh, *what*?" Andrew asked again.

Lily laughed and faux-bopped him on the arm. "You guys know I've been making a lot of positive changes lately. Working on my business degree, upping my game with my recipes and cooking techniques at the Maverick Manor, really thinking about my future plans, saying yes to experiences I normally wouldn't." She didn't add that those yeses included one to Viv Dalton when she'd asked if Lily wanted to throw her name into the Crawford brothers dating pool. But it was a great example of how she'd gone from *Nah, but thanks* to *Why not?* "So I wanted a new look to reflect who I feel like on the inside. I'm not the scrappy tomboy chasing after you guys in the woods with an insect net anymore."

"Well, you'll always be that girl," her dad said. "But you're this woman, too."

Aww, her father had tears in his eyes. Now he was going to make Lily cry and she would mess up her mascara. She'd practiced applying it four times last night until she got it right, somewhere between natural and enhanced.

"You look flipping amazing, Lil," Andrew said.

"Beautiful," Bobby agreed with a bow.

"You know I like to rib you," Ryan added, "but I have to agree. Wow."

She grinned, thrilled with the response. "Thanks, guys. That means a lot. I'm all dressed up with somewhere to go." *Yes, I am! And look out, Xander.* She couldn't wait for his reaction.

Andrew glanced at his watch. "Speaking of the dance, I need to go pick up Heidi. See you all there."

"Want a ride, Lil?" Ryan asked. "I didn't even think you were going or I would have asked earlier. Bobby and I are picking up a couple friends, then heading over."

"I'll take my car," she said. "But thanks." The Hunt brothers headed out, and Lily breathed a sigh of relief, glad to not be under the microscope any longer.

"Should *I* go?" her father asked. "Dances aren't usually my thing, but..."

Lily felt her eyes widen. "You should!"

"Well, if you're going and look like a princess, I could certainly put on a nice shirt and comb this rat's nest on my head and sway to a country tune or two. Say hello to some people."

Lily's heart leaped. "Go change," she said with a smile. "Maybe your blue shirt with the Western yoke and the gray pants? Or even a pair of dark jeans?"

His eyes lit up. "Back in a jiff," he said, taking the stairs at a dash.

Lots of changes happening in the Hunt household, she thought with a smile. Her. Andrew in a serious relationship with Heidi. Bobby and Ryan in business together with their auto-mechanic shop. And now her dad, who'd dated here and there over the years but never let anything serious develop, was going to a town dance when he never had before.

Five minutes later, her dad was back downstairs, in the Western shirt and jeans Lily had suggested, and his good cowboy boots. He'd combed his hair and even added a little bit of his aftershave.

"You look great, Dad," she whispered, trying to avoid crying.

He nodded, dusting off imaginary lint from his shirt. "*We* look like a million bucks. Shall we?" he said, holding out his arm.

Lily grinned and wrapped her arm around her father's, her heart about to burst.

Xander saw her hair first. And just a swath of it because she was surrounded by people. He'd been on the lookout for Lily since he'd arrived at the dance about fifteen minutes ago, but there had been no sign of her. Now he'd caught a glimpse of that unmistakable red hair, those lush fiery tresses. There was something different about it, the bit he could see. Sleek and...sexy.

He moved closer, craning his neck around Henry Peterman, who was six foot four, built like a linebacker and blocking his vision. He went around Henry, and stopped dead in his tracks.

Whoa.

It was Lily—he was sure of it. But she looked nothing like the Lily he'd known for the past few weeks.

Damn, she cleaned up well.

Henry was saying something to her, and he saw Lily smile politely and respond, then step back. Another guy took Henry's place. Then another.

"Sorry, but I promised my first dance to someone," he heard Lily say.

That was his cue. He sure as hell *hoped* so, anyway.

"Lily?" he said strangely in the form of a question. Whoa, whoa, whoa. "You look beyond beautiful."

She smiled, those gorgeous green eyes all lit up. "Thanks. I needed a change."

"This is some change," he said. "Stunning." He stared at her, completely tongue-tied all of a sudden and unable to think of another thing to say. "Uh, I could go get us some punch. Nice night," he added. *Smooth, Xander. You're great at conversation.*

"I'd rather dance," she said, holding out her hand.

Her soft, pretty hand. She wore sparkly blue nail polish, silver bracelets jangling on her arm. He took her hand and led her over to the dance area, which was pretty crowded. The band was playing an old Shania Twain song he'd always loved, a slow one.

He barely heard the whispers around them as she slid her arms around his neck. *Is that Lily Hunt? Oh, my God, that's Lily. Holy buffalo, did you see Lily Hunt?*

"Guess I'll be getting that a lot tonight," she said, her eyes only on him.

They were practically chest to chest. So close he could see every individual freckle across her nose.

His hands were on her waist, on the soft, silky fabric of her dress. "Pretty in pink," he said. "Isn't that a movie?"

She smiled. "I've seen it at least ten times," she said, tightening her arms around his neck. She glanced around, then looked back at him. "It really is such a gorgeous night. I've heard that this dance is the town's way of saying goodbye to summer every year. I'm definitely not ready to see summer go."

"Me, either." He'd associated Lily with summer since he'd met her at the beginning of August, their first date, if it could really be called that, on a wings-and-sauce picnic in the park.

"And I love all the white lights strung in the trees," she said, staring up at the lights. "So festive and pretty."

"Like you," he said. He hoped to God he wasn't blushing because his cheeks sure were burning.

She laughed. "You're not used to seeing me like this."

"No. I could get used to it, though. I think. You looked great the way I met you. And you look great now."

She stopped swaying and stared at him, her expression...wistful. "That means a lot to me. Thank you."

They continued dancing, his throat going so dry at being this close to her, holding her, breathing in the delicious, sexy scent she wore, that he needed some punch or he'd pass out.

"How about that punch now?" he asked.

"I've love some."

He headed past throngs of people, most of whom he recognized now from town and the rancher association meeting he and his family had attended. Logan and Sarah were slow dancing at the edge of the dance area, Andrew and Heidi making out as they swayed not too far away.

Xander said hello to Luke and Eva Stockton, who owned Sunshine Farm and had turned it into this gorgeous guest ranch with a welcoming main house and cabins dotting the property. He saw a couple of his brothers talking to Nate Crawford, who owned the Maverick Manor, and his family, distant relatives of Xander's clan. A bunch of attractive women crossed his path with smiles and "save me a dance, will you, cowboy?" Yes, two had actually said exactly that. He finally made it to the punch and downed a cup, then poured two more and headed back over to where he'd left Lily.

Except she wasn't there.

He should have known better than to leave her alone! Of course she'd been surrounded by men the minute he'd left and was probably now dancing with someone.

The thought turned his stomach.

His gaze ran over the dance area. He saw Wilder with his arms around a pretty brunette. Finn was talking more than he was dancing with a blonde. Max Crawford was chatting up two women who looked to be his age by the buffet table. The Jones brothers—millionaire cowboys who'd moved to town over the past couple of years from Tulsa, Oklahoma—were dancing with their wives, and

Xander made a note to meet one or two of them tonight since they'd also come to Montana from out of state.

Finally, he caught a swish of the red hair. He craned his neck around two women who were looking longingly at Hunter as he was deep in conversation with their nearest ranch neighbor, and yes, there Lily was. Dancing.

With Knox.

What?

It wasn't a slow song, so his brother didn't have his arms around her. And Lily's arms were up in the air at the moment as she laughed at something Sarah, dancing next to her with Logan, said.

Now Knox was whispering something in her ear. Lily laughed and touched Knox's arm.

A red-hot burst of anger swelled in his gut. Knox had had his chance to date Lily and had opted out. *So move along, buddy.*

He marched over with the two cups of punch, someone's elbow almost knocking them out of his hands. "Hey, Lily," he said with a fast glare at his brother. "I have our punch."

"Oh, great!" Lily said. "I'm so thirsty! All this dancing."

"None for me?" Knox asked with too much amusement.

Xander narrowed his eyes at his brother.

Knox chuckled at what had to be the murderous expression on Xander's face. "I was just apologizing again to Lily for how I acted a few weeks ago. The date that wasn't. I was telling her all about Dad's master plan to get us all hitched and how the whole idea made me nuts after I'd already agreed on a date."

"I completely understand," Lily said. "And besides,

I got to meet Xander," she added, those beautiful green eyes looking straight into his.

"I'll go say hi to Nate," Knox said. "Thanks for the dance, Lily." He smiled and walked away, sending an infuriating wink at Xander.

Lily took one of the cups of punch and held it up. "A toast."

He raised his, as well. "To?"

"To change," she said, holding his gaze.

Dammit. She had him there. Change, progress, forward movement made the world go around. Stagnancy was a slow death. Case in point: Xander moving to Montana. He might have stayed back in Dallas, stewing in his bitterness. Instead, he'd opted for an entirely new state, a new life, and he'd met Lily. A woman he couldn't stop thinking about.

"Change is good," he agreed.

They clinked cups and he watched her drink, tossing back her head, her long, creamy neck so kissable-looking.

"Thanks for this," she said. They put the cups down on a tray of empties on a table, then headed toward the buffet, where there were light appetizers and tiny sandwiches.

"Must be hard to eat anyone else's food but yours when you're the best cook in town," he said, popping a mini quiche in his mouth.

She laughed. "That is some serious high praise. Thank you. But I'm hardly the best. All the cooks at the Manor are amazing. And Sarah and I had lunch in Kalispell that blew me away. I had no idea vegetable soup could be that good."

"Maybe we could go check out one of the restaurants

in Kalispell sometime," he said. "I'd love some Thai food. Or really good Italian."

"Are you asking me on a date, Xander Crawford?" she asked. "Or are we just friends?"

He felt his cheeks burn. "I... We're..." He gnawed the inside of his cheek. "I'll go get us more punch. Be right back."

The minute he left he realized that by the time he got back, she'd likely be dancing with someone else. *That is what you get, idiot*, he chastised himself. *"I... We're." Stammer, stammer, stammer. Jeez. What the hell was that?*

But he had no idea what he meant it as. Date. Friends. He just knew he wanted her to himself.

He hurried over the five feet to the punch bowl, filled two cups and yup, when he got back, Lily was dancing with some guy in a straw cowboy hat. He had a good inch on Xander, too, which bugged him.

At least it wasn't a slow dance.

The song ended and he saw Lily smile at her partner and dash away—right toward him.

"Why do I keep leaving you by your lonesome?" he asked.

"Because you have to torture yourself before you accept that there is something going on between us, Xander Crawford."

"Say how you really feel," he said with a smile.

"Hey, this is the new me. The real me. We're at a dance on a beautiful summer night. I'm in this pretty pink dress. You have on that gorgeous brown Stetson. My favorite Dierks Bentley song is playing right now. Seems like just the place to see what's what."

He handed her the punch, feeling like he'd been

socked in the stomach. She was 100 percent right. They downed the drinks, tossed the cups and hit the dance floor.

The moment her hands slid around his neck, he knew he wasn't letting her go again, wasn't letting her out of his sight.

"So what's this about an old diary you and your brothers found buried in your bedroom?" she asked, looking up at him. "I overheard Logan and Sarah talking about it. You guys found it under the floorboards?"

"Funny, I was just thinking about the diary earlier tonight. It's on my bedside table—locked. I tried to get it open with a letter opener, but I need something smaller. Plus, should I really be opening it? I don't know."

"Whose is it?" she asked, her hands both hot and cool on his neck.

He shrugged. "No idea. Someone must have hidden it under the floorboard to keep it from prying eyes and either forgot it when they moved or wanted it buried forever. I really don't know. There's a letter *A* on the cover of it. It's jewel-encrusted and was probably all fancy and expensive when it was new."

"An old jewel-encrusted locked diary!" Lily said. "Something so romantic about that! I wonder whose it could be."

"Don't mean to eavesdrop," Nate Crawford said from behind Lily. A tall, good-looking man around forty, Nate was dancing with his wife, Callie. "If it looks really old and has an A on the cover, it probably belongs to someone in the Abernathy family—that's where the Ambling A ranch originally got its name. The Abernathys left town a generation ago, though."

"Wow," Lily said after Nate and Callie excused themselves to the buffet table. "It would be great if you could get it back to an Abernathy. Imagine the family stories written in the diary."

"Or family secrets," Xander said.

"Those, too. Still would be so wonderful to return it."

He nodded. "I'll ask around about the Abernathys."

The song changed, a slow one this time, and Xander found himself pulling Lily a bit closer.

"If that's okay," he whispered.

"Oh, it's more than okay."

He breathed in the flowery scent of her hair. He could stand here holding her forever.

"Cutting in," said Henry, the huge linebacker of a cowboy. He practically knocked Xander out of the way to get to Lily.

"Her dance card is full, sorry," Xander snapped.

Lily stared at Xander, crossing her arms over her chest.

"Say what now?" Henry asked, looking confused.

"Lily promised all her dances to *me*," Xander explained.

Now Lily's stare turned into a glare—at Xander.

Henry shrugged. "Oh. You two are a couple? I didn't know. Sorry." He left, walking up to a pretty blonde standing at the edge of the dance area.

Yeah, that's right.

"I didn't get a chance to tell Henry that he misunderstood," Lily said, raising an eyebrow.

"Misunderstood what?" he asked, not liking where this was headed.

"That we're a couple. We're just *friends*. Isn't that what you keep saying? Of course that means I can't promise *all* my dances to a buddy, Xander. You understand, right?"

Grrr. "I… We…"

Now there was merriment in those flashing green eyes. "That didn't work out too well for you before."

She was right. It didn't. And he was done with all that. Lily. His Lily.

He tipped up her chin and kissed her. Hard and soft. Passionately. One hand stayed at her waist as the other went into those lush red strands.

And dammit, there was that parade clanging in his head again. Cymbals. Marching band. Someone singing hallelujah.

They were *a lot* more than just friends.

"Well, I guess he wasn't mistaken," Lily whispered.

Chapter Ten

Ooh la la, Lily thought, wrapped in Xander's arms, his soft, warm lips on hers. *Make this kiss last forever.*

"Can a guy cut in?"

She peeled open one eye to see Xander glaring at a cowboy in a white cowboy boots. "Sorry, but we're kissing here," Xander said.

"Yeah, I know," the guy said, wriggling his eyebrows.

"Ew?" Lily said, grimacing at the creep.

Xander made a fist. "Want to know *this*?"

"Possessive dudes are out," the guy said, shaking his head as he walked away.

A beautiful breeze swept through Lily's hair just then, and the creep was forgotten. All she saw was Xander's handsome face and his dark eyes. All she felt were stirrings she'd never experienced before. All she wanted was to be alone with him.

"Maybe we should go kiss somewhere more private," she whispered.

"In total agreement," he whispered back.

He took her hand and led her along the edges of the crowd, craning his neck for a good spot where they could be alone. But everywhere they looked, people or couples had taken over, even on the far side of the barn, where a pair of teenagers was making out, both of them giggling as she and Xander popped their heads around and said, "Sorry."

"There's always the Ambling A," Lily said. Boldly. Very boldly.

Those dark eyes of his locked on hers. He knew exactly what she meant.

And she did mean that. She wanted to be alone with Xander Crawford. In his bedroom. In his bed.

"It's closer than my house," she rushed to add. "And who knows when my dad might head home. Your father looks like he's having too good a time to leave anytime soon." She nodded her head over to the buffet table, where Max Crawford held court with four women.

"Nice to see him getting out and enjoying himself," Xander said. He seemed almost grateful for the reprieve in their conversation. The change of subject.

Because they both knew if they made love tonight, there would be no turning back.

"My dad, too," she said. Peter Hunt was pouring a cup of punch for a woman Lily recognized from the circulation desk at the library. *Good for you, Dad*, she thought with a smile.

Oh, wait, she thought. She'd given her dad a ride here so she needed to tell him she was leaving for a bit. He

had a key to her car so could just drive himself home
if need be.

For a bit? Hopefully they'd be gone for hours.

She pulled out her phone and sent her dad at text:
Going for a ride with Xander. He'll drop me home so
feel free to take my car home.

He sent back a kiss and heart emoji, then a smiley
face. Have fun. And yes—too much fun.

Oh, Dad, she thought with a smile as she put her
phone away. Always so supportive.

"So," Xander said. "The Ambling A."

She nodded. Twice.

He took her hand and led her to where a zillion cars
and pickups were parked. "I wisely parked in a place
where I could get out easily," he said as he opened the
door of his silver truck for her. "I thought I'd be leaving
in a half hour. Alone."

"Surprises are great, aren't they?"

"This one sure is," he whispered so low that she
wasn't entirely sure he'd said that, but thought he had.

They headed out toward the ranch, the radio playing
low, the windows halfway open to let in the warm and
breezy summer night air. In ten minutes they were at the
Ambling A, not a car in sight.

"It's our lucky night, for sure," he said. "No prying
eyes." He helped her out of the truck and took her hand,
leading her into the house.

She'd been here recently, cooked in the kitchen, eaten
at the dining room table, talked and laughed with all the
Crawfords, and now the house felt comfortable and familiar and dear. He gestured toward the stairs, and up
they went.

Oh God, oh God, oh God. Suddenly a dream she'd had

for three weeks was about to come true and she could hardly believe it.

The overhead light was off in Xander's bedroom, just the table lamp casting a soft glow over the bed with its blue-and-white quilt and four pillows.

Xander closed the door behind him—and locked it. "Finally. A little privacy. A lot of privacy, I amend."

She smiled. "I'm not used to all that attention. I'm not sure if I liked it or not, to be honest." Debuting her new look at the dance was half fun, half the opposite of fun. At first, the reaction had been welcome. But when guys started buzzing around her just because she suddenly looked "hot," to use the word one cowboy had whispered in her ear as he'd walked past, Lily had had enough.

"I didn't have this 'Cinderella' night so that I could dance with fifty guys or have more dates than all you Crawfords combined," Lily said. "I just wanted my outside to reflect my inside."

"I think I know what you mean. I've always seen you, Lily Hunt. No matter what clothes you're wearing or if you smell like flowers or garlic, I see you. And I've always admired that person."

She stepped toward him until she had him backed against the door, her arms snaking around his neck. "I know. Even when things got awkward on that first date, I *knew*. I caught you by surprise, Xander Crawford."

He grinned. "You sure as hell did. Kapow!" he added, faux-punching himself in the jaw with his right hand, which he then slid around her waist.

She leaned up on her tiptoes to lift her face toward his and he met her in a kiss that almost had her knees wobbling. Good thing he picked her up in his arms, never breaking that kiss, and carried her to the bed.

She was on Xander's bed. Oh God. Oh God. Oh God. Yesssss!

A thousand butterflies let loose in her stomach just then.

Lily wasn't a virgin—but her two short-term relationships, where both guys had been as fumbling as she was, hadn't exactly taught her the art of sex. When she was nineteen and had decided to finally lose her virginity to her first real boyfriend, she'd summoned the courage to ask a close girlfriend how you knew what to do. Her friend had told her she wouldn't have to think about it at all, that desire would lead the way, and she could respond in any way that felt right and natural. Lily had thought that was good advice and it had actually made her feel more equipped. Her first time, she'd felt more anticipation than desire and the experience hadn't exactly been all that comfortable. With the second relationship, the guy was so shy that she had to lead the way. So nothing remotely like TV or movie sex had ever happened in her life.

She had a good feeling that Xander knew what he was doing.

He lay beside her on the bed, on his side, his hands caressing her hair, her face, her back. And then he was kissing her again, and she closed her eyes, almost unable to process all the emotions swirling inside her. She moved closer against him, kissing him with equal passion. There was too much clothing between them, she thought, her hands in his thick, wavy dark hair.

"A little help with the zipper?" she asked as she sat up, glancing at him.

The grin he gave her made her laugh. "My pleasure," he said, kneeling behind her.

He unzipped. Then he slowly moved the spaghetti straps off her shoulders. He kissed the sides of her neck, her collarbone, and she shimmied out of the dress, never so grateful for having bought new undergarments.

"Ooh, that's sexy," he said, taking in the blush-colored lace demi bra and matching bikini panties. "You're sexy."

Lily Hunt, sexy. No one had ever said *that* before.

She went for his belt buckle, and again, the happy surprise on his gorgeous face emboldened her even more.

"I've always said, you're a woman who knows what she wants and goes for it," he said as he kicked off his jeans and she unbuttoned his shirt.

And kissed her way down his chest.

Who *was* this woman?

One of the best parts of tonight was that she knew it wasn't the makeover giving her confidence. It was the way Xander Crawford made her *feel*. The real Lily had truly come out of her shell, every last bit of her.

In less than a minute, they were both naked. Lily felt his gaze on her, and she didn't feel exposed or shy or awkward. She only felt desire. And desirable.

Xander reached into his bedside table drawer and out came a little square foil packet.

And then he was kissing her again, his hands everywhere, his lips everywhere. The moment they became one, Lily gasped and lost all ability to think beyond how incredibly good she felt, how happy she was.

How in love.

Lily's eyes fluttered open, and she almost pulled the quilt over her head to go back to sleep when she remembered: this wasn't her bed. And she wasn't alone.

A smile spread across her face as she turned her head

slightly to the right to see if she'd dreamed the whole thing.

Because it had been a dream. Wow.

But nope, Xander Crawford was right there, fast asleep. He didn't snore, either.

She watched his chest rise and fall, rise and fall, mesmerized by his pecs and the dark swirls of hair. She wished she could stay in this bed all day—all the days of her life—but she had to sneak out before a whole bunch of Crawfords woke up and caught her creeping down the stairs.

She gave Xander one last look, drank in every gorgeous bit of him, then picked up her pink dress and slipped it on, put on her shoes, found her little beaded purse and slung that over her torso. She wanted to kiss Xander goodbye but didn't want to wake him, so she tiptoed to the door and pulled it open as gently as she could.

Lily peered out left and right. The coast was clear. She dashed down the stairs and was almost at the bottom when she realized she'd ridden here with Xander.

Which meant she was going back upstairs. Very quietly. She'd have to wake Xander, after all.

Which she was now looking forward to.

Unless things would be weird? Awkward? The morning after with its bright light? She turned around and took the first step back up, suddenly not wanting to move too quickly.

What if Xander regretted their night together?

She was barely on the fourth step up when the front door to the Ambling A opened and Lily froze, her back to it. She had no idea who it was who'd come in.

Someone who'd also had a good time at the dance, clearly.

"That red hair can mean only one woman," the male voice said. "Hey, Lily. How are ya?"

She tried to force the embarrassed grimace off her face and turned around. It was Wilder, Xander's youngest brother. He looked a bit rumpled but otherwise as handsome as all the Crawfords were with his slightly long brown hair and the piercing dark eyes.

"I'm well," she said, then rolled her eyes at herself. Could she sound more stiff? "I'm doing just great. How are *you*? Have a good time at the dance?" The questions rushed out of her mouth to put the focus back on him.

"Oh, yeah," he drawled. "Almost too good a time." He took off his cowboy boots and left them by the door. "So you're in the same clothes you were in last night, but you're just getting here?" he asked.

Thank you, Lord! Because she was on her way up the stairs, Wilder must have thought she'd just gotten here.

"Long story," she said, figuring Wilder Crawford was not really interested in her love life.

"Let me guess. You had too much of the spiked version of the punch, fell asleep under a tree, woke up with leaves in your hair, then remembered you promised your buddy Xander you'd give him a cooking lesson and so here you are."

Um, no. She wanted to tell him she wasn't the kind of person who passed out under trees at parties, but she wanted to run with the idea that she hadn't just tried to sneak out of the house after spending the most amazing night of her life here.

"Well, I see I made you blush, and honestly, Lily? Don't worry about it. If you knew *half* the crazy times my brothers and I have had, then you'd really have something to blush about. And I'm not even talking about the women coming and going. Ask Xander to tell you the story of the time he had three dates in one night. People say I'm the wild Crawford who lives up to my name? Xander has us all beat for notches on the bedpost. Including here in Rust Creek Falls. He's not even the tallest of us. Personally, I don't get it..."

Her stomach dropped.

What?

As Wilder went on about how much each Crawford could bench-press, Lily tuned him out, suddenly wishing she hadn't given him the impression that she and Xander were "just friends."

Now instead of being embarrassed at getting caught, she wanted to run away. Maybe bawl.

"Well, I'll go wake Xander. Bye!" she croaked out and dashed up the stairs.

"If you're making pancakes, make at least ten for me!" he called up.

Oh God. Did everyone hear that? Had Wilder woken up the whole house?

She raced into Xander's room, shutting and locking the door behind her, her heart beating so loud she was sure it was what woke Xander.

"You've got too many clothes on," he said, propping up in bed. "You've *got* clothes on."

Calm down, Lily. Don't go all just-how-many-women-have-been-in-this-bed *on him. Everything that happened before last night was the past.* Last night was a new beginning for them both.

Right?

She could feel the exact spot her heart was bruised. Dead center. Was she another "notch on the bedpost" as Wilder had unwittingly put it?

Back in high school, the guys had had a brief sickening game they'd dubbed "least likely." Whoever got the most girls they were least likely to kiss to kiss them, won. Won what, Lily didn't know. Unearned respect from the idiots, she guessed.

That week, ten guys, most from the football team, had asked Lily if she wanted to take a walk—with a gleam in their eyes. The first time, she'd been so bewildered that one of the hottest, most popular guys in school had sort of asked her out that she'd said yes, without any idea if she actually liked him or not. Turns out they had nothing much to say on their ten-minute walk, but all he'd been after was a kiss on the lips. Once he got it, he'd said, *Booya!* And run back toward the school. The next morning, Lily had heard a group of cheerleaders talking about the bet and how skater dudes were suddenly asking them out—as if.

Lily had said no to the next nine guys who'd "asked her out."

And had had a hard time trusting in a man being attracted to her *for* her ever since.

But with Xander, she knew he was. She knew it and believed it the way she knew her own name.

So forget the past. Everything is about now. Now, now, now.

Never mind that *now*, she felt very unsure of herself. No. Not of herself. Of *them*.

"Wait," Xander said, frowning. "Were you about to leave?"

"I actually did leave but got halfway downstairs when I remembered I didn't drive here. So I'm stranded."

He grinned. "Guess that means you'll have to come back to bed." He held up the side of the quilt.

"I ran into Wilder on the stairs," she said, arms across her chest. "At first I thought he caught me doing the famous walk of shame, but turns out he thinks we're just friends, so he gave me an earful about the women who've come and gone from this very room since you've been in Rust Creek Falls."

"Wilder talks too much," he said, shaking his head.

"You were supposed to say 'fake news.'"

His expression softened as he realized he'd confirmed her worst fears.

"I won't lie to you, Lily. I've had a couple of very short-term...experiences. Just the first couple weeks after I moved here and felt really overwhelmed by everything."

Her arms fell to her sides and felt like they weighed a hundred pounds each. Like her heart right now.

"I was so upset about what happened back in Dallas," he continued, reaching for his pants. "I wanted to forget and so I went out a lot those first couple weeks. Not even here in town, but in the surrounding towns to be more anonymous."

"You're my third lover," she blurted out. Then immediately wished she could take it back. She dropped down on the edge of the bed, facing away from him. "The first guy? There was no second time. I think we both just wanted to get our virginities over with and it wasn't exactly a spiritual experience." She sighed. "The second guy and I lasted a few weeks but we didn't have any chemistry except when it came to discussing pastry—we met in a baking class." She stood up, then dropped back down. "My point is that I don't have much experience in any of this. And you clearly do."

"Well, I've got seven years on you," he said, getting up

and pulling on his jeans. "I'm thirty years old. Friends of mine have been long married with two kids by my age."

She turned to face him, stunned silent for a moment by the sight of the morning light hitting the muscled planes of his chest. Just hours ago, her hands had explored every millimeter of that chest. His entire body.

And now…everything was wrong.

And everything hurt.

He walked around his bed to his dresser and pulled a blue T-shirt out of a drawer. "One of the reasons why I was so hesitant about us," he said, putting on the shirt, "was because I know what getting emotionally involved leads to."

Dammit. Was he going to do this? Had she actually set this conversation in motion? Oh God.

No. Wait one minute. She was not about to blame herself for talking about reality. The truth. If he wanted to revert back to the guy who hid from life—and love— well, that wasn't her fault.

It just happened to hurt like hell.

Crud.

Had she really thought her night with Xander was going somewhere? That he'd suddenly be over his past and trust in the world again?

Yes, she had thought so.

Maybe because she was as young and experienced at life as he'd said she was.

"I thought there was more between us," she said. "Was I wrong?"

He held her gaze for a second, then turned away, his attention out the window. "You weren't wrong, Lily. But I guess this conversation just brought up all the reminders that—"

He stopped and sat down on the edge of the bed, running a hand through his hair.

"Reminders that…?" she prompted.

"That I'm jaded and bitter. And you're young and hopeful and idealistic and have your whole beautiful life ahead of you."

"That's total bunk, Xander Crawford. You're just scared spitless that you feel more for me than you intended. And so you're pushing me away."

"Lily—"

But again, he stopped talking.

"When you find someone truly special, you don't let them go, Xander. Do you realize how rare it is?"

"Is it?" he asked.

"Oh, so I'm just a dime a dozen?" She glared at him, grateful the anger was edging out the hurt. No, wait. There the hurt was. Punching back for control.

At least the anger was keeping her from crying. That she'd do in private.

"This wasn't how I envisioned the morning going," he said, standing up. "Not at all. I thought we'd make love three more times, then I'd sneak you into the shower with me, and then whisk you off to the Gold Rush for scrambled eggs and home fries and bacon and a lot of coffee and then we'd go back to my place for a repeat. That's what I thought this morning would be."

Now she did feel like crying. "I wanted that morning, too, Xander. I still want it."

"But you want a lot more than that, don't you?" he said gently.

"Hell yeah."

"I'm sorry, Lily. I messed up by kissing you in the first

place because I just couldn't resist you. And now I've made this huge mess of things. I'm very sorry."

"You're sorry for sleeping with me?" she said, her voice sounding more like a screech. This time, the anger had knocked out the hurt with a solid left jab. "How dare you!"

"Lily, no, I—"

"I need a ride home. And I'd like that ride to be *silent*."

He let out a harsh sigh and headed for the door.

Tears pricked the backs of her eyes.

Lily raced down the stairs, dimly aware of laughter coming from the direction of the kitchen. She could hear a couple of voices. She had to get out of there before anyone saw her—especially now that this really was just another notch on Xander's bedpost.

She tried hard to keep the tears from falling, but down they came. Lily flung open the door and ran out, zooming for Xander's truck. She got in, wiping away her tears. *Take a deep breath. Do. Not. Let. Him. See. You. Cry.*

By the time he got in the driver's seat, she was composed.

Do not think about last night. How you kissed at the dance. How you two drove to the Ambling A with all those feelings, romance in the air, love in the air, all your hopes coming true...

She wanted to blame it on herself for falling for Xander when he told her by his actions alone on their first date that he was going to smash her heart to smithereens.

She wanted to blame it on that blasted Wilder Crawford—and her unfortunate timing of running into him—for telling her stuff she had no business knowing. Or wanting to know.

But the blame for her feeling like she'd just been

kicked and Xander's probably feeling like hell? That was on Xander himself—and his stubbornness.

But as he started the truck and pulled out, something occurred to Lily. Something the old Lily would have thought of immediately. The new Lily had too much confidence, though, so the news flash hadn't seeped into her consciousness until now.

Maybe it had nothing to do with Xander living in the past and being stubborn.

Maybe he just didn't love her back.

Chapter Eleven

Xander pulled up in front of Lily's house, Dobby and Harry sitting outside on the porch, Harry on his back on the mat, taking in the brilliant sunshine of late August. Xander wanted to run up and rub that furry little belly, feel Harry's soft-as-silk floppy ears, talk to her dad, ask her brothers how things were going at the auto mechanic business, where they'd fixed his brother Finn's brake issue the other day. He even wanted to hang out with Andrew and hear how things were with Heidi. Xander's first fix-up.

At least he brought love to someone. Two someones.

Please don't rush out of the truck until I get to say something, he thought, but couldn't make himself speak the words. He didn't know *what* he wanted to say.

I'm sorry didn't cut it. There was so much more to say but he couldn't put words to it.

He turned off the ignition and turned to face her. "Lily."

But nothing else came out of his mouth.

She waited. She tilted her head. Waited some more. Then she said, "Everything between us led to last night, Xander. And last night was something beautiful. Personally, I think you're crazy for turning your back on it. But if that's your choice, I guess I have to respect that." She cleared her throat and reached for the door.

"Last night *was* beautiful," he said.

"And?" she prompted.

"And…maybe it's better we cool it now rather than someone gets run over by a Mack truck down the road."

"You're the only one driving that truck, Xander," she said—between gritted teeth. Then she got out of the car and stalked to the door in her pink dress, the dogs jumping up to greet her.

He watched her pet both of them and bury her face in their fur, then hurry inside, the dogs behind her.

The door closed and he felt so bereft.

He felt *something* for her, that was not in doubt.

He started the truck and drove toward the Ambling A. A hard day's work would help set his mind at ease by taking his brain off Lily completely. But by the time he got to the ranch, his mind was a jumble. Memories of last night, of what it was like to make love to Lily, to be one with her, how complete he'd felt, kept jabbing at him.

He didn't want to feel complete, though. That was the damn problem. He'd felt complete in Dallas with Britney to the point that he was going to propose.

And wham. Knocked upside the head and left for dead.

A little dramatic, but that was how it felt.

He needed a walk, and the now overcast morning suited his mood. He'd survey the miles of fence line out past the barn, see if any part of it needed repair. He wrapped a tool kit around his hips, then headed out on foot to the fence, a good mile away. As he neared it, he could see his brother Knox with his tools, working on a long gap in the wiring.

"Guess we had the same idea for this morning," Xander said.

Knox glanced up. "Glad you're here. I could use a hand." Knox used a tool to stretch the wire, and Xander wrapped the wire around and around the next section to secure it. "I was riding fence when I noticed it." He glanced for Xander's horse. "You walked all the way out here?"

"A lot on my mind," Xander said.

"Yeah, ditto. But after working so hard there's no way I'd want to hoof it back, so I brought the trusty steed." He nodded up at the beautiful brown mare.

"Still mad at me for dancing with your chef?" Knox asked. But Xander could tell his brother wasn't kidding.

"Yes, actually. Dammit." He sighed and ran a hand through his hair. "Not dammit that you danced with her. Dammit that she *is* 'my chef' and I'm screwing it up. I really care about Lily. I more than care about her. I just don't *want* to. If that makes any sense."

"Unfortunately, it does. All part of our legacy."

Their legacy. The six of them rarely talked about their upbringing, and he figured that was what Knox was referring to.

"With our family past, who the hell wouldn't be wary of love and marriage and all that stuff?" Knox asked, not looking up.

Xander didn't know all that much about their mother, but she'd been considerably younger than their father, jumping into the marriage not long after they'd started dating. And he knew that Sheila Crawford had left Max and their six young children for another man—and never looked back.

If his mother had been able to do that, anyone could. Britney sure had.

So why wouldn't Lily? When she had her whole life ahead of her at just twenty-three?

She was probably right when she'd said, in so many words, that the past was running his life, that it had too tight a grip on him. But right now, that grip was stronger than hers.

"You'll figure it out," Knox said, shaking him out of his thoughts.

"Meaning?"

Knox tightened the final piece of wire. "Either Lily will win out or the family legacy will. Logan got lucky. Maybe you will, too."

Huh. He hadn't really thought of it that way before. But he knew luck had nothing to do with Logan settling down with Sarah and baby Sophia. *Love* had won out.

For some crazy reason, he felt a little better than he had when he'd first walked out here. Maybe because he forgot that love *could* win.

Lily was glad she'd had to work today. One of today's specials was the Aegean pizza she'd introduced to the menu, an immediate hit, and she'd made at least thirty of them since the Manor had opened for lunch. She had her eye on the six in her oven as she sliced chicken and chopped garlic and green peppers for the next batch, trying to not pop all the delicious feta cheese in her mouth before she ran out. Her waiters had reported on where her diners were from, but she couldn't exactly add barbecue sauce or cayenne pepper or roasted chestnut shavings to the Aegean pizza without ruining it, so she kept her special additions to the other entrées. She'd made several big pots of minestrone soup, adding a bit of this and that to it to bring her diners a bit of home. Five tables had ordered servings of the soup to go, so that had brought a smile.

And she wasn't feeling much like smiling today.

When she left for the day and arrived home, she didn't even bother going upstairs to relax or take a bath to soothe her weary muscles and mind. She hit the kitchen. She had a few clients around town who loved her cooking at the Manor and hired her to make special-occasion meals or texted her that they were ill and could she drop off what they were craving. This evening, she was making split pea soup with carrots and tiny bits of ham for Monty Parster, her seventy-five-year-old widowed client who had a cold. Monty was usually robust and volunteered in the library, putting away books that had been returned, and Lily adored him. She'd make him a pot of his favorite feel-better soup on the house.

"And this is the living room," she heard her dad suddenly say, along with two sets of footsteps. One with a definite heel.

"Why do I smell something amazing?" a woman's voice asked.

Oooh, did her dad have a date over?

"That must be my daughter, Lily. She's a chef at the Maverick Manor. Best cook in the county, maybe even the state. Or the country!"

"Well, whatever she's making certainly smells like it," the woman said.

Lily liked her already.

"Lil?" Peter Hunt asked as he poked his head inside the kitchen.

"Hi, Dad," she said with a smile, stirring the pea soup as it simmered. It *did* smell good.

He pushed open the door, and behind him was an attractive woman around his age with shoulder-length dark hair and warm hazel eyes. "Lil, this Charlotte McKown. We met at the dance last night."

Lily extended her hand. "It's so nice to meet you. The dance was wonderful. I must have eaten ten of those little ham-and-cheese quiches."

"Me, too," Charlotte said. "And a little too many of the mini raspberry cheesecakes."

Lily laughed. "Yup, same here."

As her dad escorted Charlotte to the powder room so she could freshen up before their dinner at the Manor, Lily gave the soup a taste and declared it done and perfect. She shut off the burner just as her dad came back into the kitchen, a big smile on his face.

"Our first date was breakfast at the Gold Rush Diner," he whispered. "We were so full of French toast and pancakes and bacon that we skipped lunch."

"So this is an all-day date?" Lily asked with a grin. "Dad, I'm thrilled."

"We have a lot to talk about. She's widowed, too. And has four grown kids just like me. She takes Pilates and does yoga and volunteers in the clinic. She's a great person."

"Sure sounds like it," Lily said.

They could hear the powder room door opening, so her dad kissed her on the cheek and dashed out.

Lily laughed. Her dad sure seemed to be falling in love.

Next would be Ryan and Bobby. They'd probably each met someone at the dance, too.

Oh well, she thought. At least most of the Hunts were happy. She carefully poured the soup into a big container, put a lid on it, grabbed some crackers and sourdough bread and then headed out to her car.

A few minutes later, she was in Mr. Parster's little Cape Cod–style house. He sat in a recliner with a cro-cheted throw over him, a box of tissues beside him. Lily prepared a tray with the soup, which was still piping hot, and the crackers and bread, and a glass of lemon water, and brought it out to him, placing it on a table that wheeled right over his lap.

"Ah, my favorite split pea," he said. "Did I ever tell you that you make it just like my wife did?"

She smiled. "You gave me her recipe. It's my favorite version, too. I make it for the Manor, too, and it's always a hit."

He took a spoonful. "Ahhh," he said. "So good. And trust me, it's you, not the recipe. My second-oldest daughter made this for me the last time I was sick, and I tell you, it was terrible! Something was just missing. Not that I told her that!"

Lily smiled. She adored Mr. Parster.

He took another spoonful, then nibbled on a piece of the sourdough bread, which Lily had made herself as well yesterday. "I'm sure that hoity-toity Maverick Manor pays you a fortune, but you could be making a killing by going into business for yourself as a personal chef. I'd hire you to make every meal for me. Good thing I actually like to cook myself or I'd go bankrupt. Oh, speaking of, will you be teaching another cooking class for seniors? I'm interested in Asian cooking."

"Wait," she said. "You think I could make a living as a personal chef? Here in Rust Creek Falls?"

"Are you kidding? You'd rake it in. Those who are sick. Single parents. Working parents. Dolt bachelors who never learned to crack an egg. Special occasions. Parties. Work events. Trust me, everyone knows when Lily Hunt is working at the Manor and they go those days."

"Really?" she asked. Mr. Parster was a bit of a busybody who was on at least five town boards, so it was possible he was in the know.

"I don't go around blowing smoke," he said. "Anyway, just an idea." He ate two more spoonfuls. "Heavenly. How do you get these carrots so soft and delicious?"

She laughed. "I'm very happy you love the soup. And thank you for the compliment. Well, the rest of the soup is in the fridge with reheating instructions. Want me to stick around? Make you some tea?"

"Nah," he said. "My other daughter is coming with a German chocolate cake. She's a much better cook than Karly. Don't tell her I said that."

Lily laughed. "Sworn to secrecy."

As she headed out to her car, she couldn't stop thinking about what he'd said. Personal chef? She'd thought about having her own restaurant one day, something small to start, to learn the business and grow as a chef. Or her own catering shop for events. But being a personal chef hadn't really occurred to her. Made-to-order dishes for individuals and families? And businesses and events, too? Hmm. A more personal touch.

She could have her own business doing what she loved.

She could even turn her little gift for reminding people of their best memories and home into her work.

Lily's Home Cookin'.

Her heart leaped and pulse sped up. Yes! She would start her own home-based food business as a personal chef. She could offer meal-prep kits and ready-made dishes and make herself available for parties and events. She could be all things to all stomachs!

Lily's Home Cookin'.

This time, when tears pricked her eyes it was because she was overcome with joy. Her mother would be proud of her. She knew it.

She drove home, thinking about the business plan she'd need to create. Using what she'd learned in school, doing some more research online and really homing in on what she envisioned for her business, Lily could even approach the bank about a small business loan. She wouldn't need incredible overhead to start, but she'd need decent padding for the ingredients she'd need, cookware, containers and labels, advertising, an accountant and her own space.

Yes. It was time to find her own home, a condo or small house with a good-sized, modern kitchen. Her dad would understand and he'd also be proud of her.

All that settled in her mind, she turned on the radio, planning to sing along at the top of her lungs to her favorite station, but there was a commercial on. Of course.

"Northwest Montana's Best Chef Contest this weekend in Kalispell," the radio host was saying. "Dead-

line to enter is tonight at midnight. See details online at
NW Montana's Best Chef Contest dot com. Good luck,
local cooks! Ten thousand big ones would even get me
to enter—if I could cook a burger without charring it
to death."

One of her favorite songs came on, but Lily snapped
off the radio. *Ten thousand dollars?*

Ten. Thousand. Dollars.

More than enough money to get her business off the
ground, pay first and last month's rent on her own place
and have some cushion for emergencies.

She had to enter that contest. She had to *win* that
contest!

Lily pulled into the driveway and rushed inside, dashing upstairs to her desk and opening her laptop. She
typed the name of the contest into the search engine,
and there it was. According to the site, the first round
was an elimination event on Friday night—all hopefuls
would make the same dish, based on the same recipe
and the same ingredients. The top ten entrants would
move on to round two. Three finalists would be chosen
to move on and after the next round, one winner would
be named. And awarded ten grand and the right to call
herself Northwest Montana's Best Chef. *Note*, she read.
*All entrants must bring an assistant who will aid only
with prep, help fetch ingredients, cookware, utensils
and plates during the competition, and help with time
management.*

Wait—*what?*

An assistant?

She raced out of her room into Andrew's. Not home.
Neither were Bobby or Ryan. She texted all three.

Busy this weekend? I need an assistant for a cooking contest in Kalispell.

Within fifteen minutes, she had a "no can do" from them all. Andrew had a special orientation at the academy. Bobby and Ryan were booked solid at the auto-mechanic shop. And she already knew her dad had two special dates planned with Charlotte because he'd texted her so while she'd been in the powder room during their dinner out.

Sarah had a baby—no way could Lily, or would Lily, even ask her. Two other very busy girlfriends were also not likely to be available.

There *was* one other person she could ask. He might be free. And willing.

But if he said yes, could she really bear spending the weekend with him? Her heart would break a tiny bit more every time she looked at him.

She *had* to enter the contest—and win.

Which meant picking up the phone and calling Xander Crawford.

Chapter Twelve

Lily grabbed her phone, sucking in a deep breath. She punched in his number and brought the phone to her ear, her heart beating a mile a minute.

"Lily?" he asked. "Everything okay?"

"Everything's fine. I just need a favor. A big favor."

"My answer is yes," he said.

She flopped down on her bed, eyebrow raised. "You don't even know what the favor is."

"Don't need to, Lil. I'd do anything for you."

Tears stung her eyes. This time, not from joy. But from the bittersweet poke at knowing how much he cared about her—and how she'd never have him the way she wanted.

I'd do anything for you—except be in love with you or lie to you about it.

The cooking contest, she reminded herself. She had

to think only of that. "Does 'anything' include being my assistant for the weekend at the Northwest Montana's Best Chef Contest? We'd leave Friday night and return Saturday night. I know you probably can't do it—it's last minute and practically all weekend and—"

"How many aprons should I pack?" he asked. "Do I own an apron? Do I get to wear a chef's hat?"

She almost burst into tears. She had to cover her mouth with her hand and squeeze her eyes shut. That was how touched she was that he was going to help her.

"I'll bring the aprons," she managed to say. "And yes on the chef hat."

"Count me in, then," he said.

She could barely catch her breath. "Thank you, Xander. You have no idea how much this means to me to enter the contest." She told him all about her business plan, the idea for Lily's Home Cookin' and how the ten thousand would get her started and then some.

"I always said you'd run the world someday, Lil. I'm happy to help you. And honestly, any time you need something, I'm here for you. I'd do anything for you," he repeated.

Except be in love with me. Except be with me. Except commit to me.

At least she had her weekend assistant. And she knew she could trust him to work hard and fast. The time they'd spent in the kitchen at the kids' cooking class and his few cooking lessons gave him a good familiarity.

Now she'd just have to get through the weekend with total focus on the three dishes they would make instead of on the man she loved.

She could do that. She *would* do that.

"Are you free now to discuss what I'll be doing?" he asked. "I could be over in fifteen minutes."

Wait—he wanted to come over?

"You could explain to me what you'll be cooking and what I'll need to do to help, how the contest works. I don't want to be the one who ruins the whole thing for you by chopping something in the wrong dimensions."

Lily smiled. "Well, there's a website with a ton of information. But sure, why don't you come over, and we'll go over it, and work out a plan based on what I know. The actual dishes I'll be making are a surprise."

"Oh, *that's* always helpful in a competition," he said. "Right?"

"Be right over, Lil," he said.

She held the phone on her heart for the next few minutes, unable to get up, unable to think.

She could barely get through knowing the man she loved was coming over to talk about the contest. How in the heck would she get through a weekend that promised to be incredibly high stress as it was?

She just would. You *want it*, you *make it happen*. Wasn't that her motto? Sure, sometimes it *didn't* happen, à la Xander Crawford.

But it had to this weekend with the ten thousand bucks. It just had to.

A weekend away with Lily? Yes.

Helping Lily with something very important to her? Yes.

She'd get her assistant and he'd get his friend back. Win-win.

He drove over to her house, greeted by Dobby and

Harry, who ran out for their vigorous pet-downs, Lily standing in the doorway.

She wasn't in the pink dress but she still didn't look like the Lily he'd always known.

She wore very sexy jeans that molded to her body. A V-neck tank top that showed her curves. And sandals that revealed sparkly green toenails. Her gorgeous red hair was sleek and shiny and loose around her shoulders.

She looked too hot.

And man, he thought she'd looked hot before this change.

With the dogs at his shins, he headed in, trying not to stare at Lily.

"I can't thank you enough, Xander," she said. "I know we left things kind of awkward, so...just thank you."

He nodded. "Happy to help." He followed her up to her room, and she shut the door behind them. He sat down at her desk chair; she grabbed her laptop and sat cross-legged on the bed.

The bed, of course, brought back memories of the last time he saw her on a bed. In bed. Under his covers.

"So what's my role?" he asked. *Stop looking at her legs. Stop looking at her hair. Stop looking at her.*

She told him what the site said about the assistant's role. "So, you can chop veggies, gather ingredients, get me a sauté pan, and you can say, 'Lily, you have a half hour left.' But you can't do any actual cooking."

"Well, that's good because I'm pretty bad at it."

"I recall you making excellent omelets," she said. "Even Andrew remarked on how good it was."

"Nice try, Lil. But *we* took the ones that I made. They had the good ones *you* made. Remember?"

"You did a great job turning the bacon with the tongs

and getting the cheese out of the fridge," she said with a grin. "And that's pretty much your role at the competition."

He raised an eyebrow. "Except I don't know a sauté pan from a colander."

"Good point. Let's hit the kitchen and I'll give you a tutorial. You can even take notes."

He actually pulled a tiny notebook with a little pen in the spiral from his back pocket. "Of course I'll take notes. I've gotta help you win."

She got up from the bed, her gaze on him, and it took everything in him not to reach for her, to say he was sorry, that he had no idea what he was doing.

But she'd already opened the door and was waiting for him.

In the kitchen, she knelt down in front of a cabinet and pulled out a bunch of pots and pans. She put them all on the counter. "Which do you think is a sauté pan? You'd cook fish in it or chicken or make an omelet."

"Probably this one," he said, pointing at one with shallow sides. "I think."

"Correct!"

"Soup or chili or spaghetti pot?" she asked.

"I'd think it would have to be pretty high to be a spaghetti pot, and I know when my dad makes chili, it's always in some huge pot." He pointed to the pot he thought would be right.

"Correct again!" she said. "A-plus so far."

They went through all the pots and pans, then moved on to the cooking utensils, covering everything from spatulas to colanders to food processors.

"Catch!" she said, tossing a green pepper at him. "Get ready to slice, dice and chop."

He caught it after it bounced against his chest. "Catch!" he said, tossing it back.

She got it in one hand. "Catch!" she said, turning around and tossing it behind her.

"Ha, got it!" He laughed, tossing it up in the air and catching it with his left hand. "Who knew you could have so much fun with food?"

She grinned. "I did."

"You're going to win the contest. I know it."

She smiled, then sobered fast. "You really believe in me."

"Sure do. I've had your French dip. That's all I need to know."

Lily laughed and he realized how much he'd missed that beautiful sound. He wished he could always make her happy. "Well," she said, clearing her throat. "Time for the cutting lessons."

For the next hour, she showed him how to slice thin and thick, how to dice, how to peel and separate garlic cloves.

They'd been in the kitchen for three hours when she let out a giant yawn.

"Someone needs to get her cooking contest rest," he said. "What time are we leaving tomorrow?"

"I need to be there no later than six."

"I'll drive. Pick you up at four forty-five just to be safe. Better to be a half hour early than a few minutes late."

She wrapped her arms around him and kissed his cheek, and again he wanted to pull her against him and never let her go.

"Thank you so much, Xander. You are a true friend."

Friend. Buddy. Nice. Just friends. The words echoed in his head.

They were going away for the weekend. Together. Staying—he assumed—in the same room. Or was he just hoping they were?

"I guess I should book a room for myself?" he asked as he washed his hands in the sink.

"I already did. We have two single rooms but the guy taking the reservations said they were among the last rooms available. So phew."

His heart sank.

You can't have it both ways, man, he reminded himself.

Late that night, after a practice dinner on her family that they all raved about, and another half hour lying on her bed staring up at the ceiling, and another half hour going over the contest website for every detail, Lily decided to start packing. She set her suitcase on her bed and opened it, wondering what to take—for the competition *and* a weekend away with the man she was madly in love with.

For the competition, she'd wear her new jeans and tank tops and bring two light cardigans, plus her trusty lucky clogs, which were comfortable and nonslip and made her feel grounded.

For the weekend away with Xander, she'd bring the sexy underwear (because why not? Even if he never saw it, she'd know it was there) and the sleeveless little black dress and strappy sandals.

Hell yeah. You never knew.

She grabbed her phone and texted Sarah: Entering a

weekend-cooking competition in Kalispell. Guess who my assistant is?

OMG. No way.

As friends. But hopeful.

Me too! Wow! Good luck on both fronts!

Just after she sent back a smiley face emoji, someone knocked on her door. At her "come in!" her brother Andrew poked his head in.

"Got a minute?" he asked.

"Sure."

He came in and sat down on her desk chair. "I just wanted to say thanks, Lil. Everything is because of you."

She put down her phone and stared at Andrew. "What's because of me?"

"Me being really happy. Having Heidi in my life. Dad dating for the first time in forever. I think he's in love."

Lily smiled. "Dad does seem really happy. I met Charlotte. She seems great. But how is either relationship my doing? I didn't introduce you to Heidi or Dad to Charlotte."

"Still it's *because* of you. When I watched you enroll in school for business administration, it spurred me to really think about what I wanted for my future—and I enrolled in the police academy. Then you made pals with a Crawford, and I got the cojones to ask him if he'd pass my name and number to any date he thought would work out. And I met Heidi. You said you were going to the annual dance that you never went to and Dad goes and falls in love. It's all thanks to you. You made really positive changes in your life and now we're doing that, too."

Her heart pinged. "Andrew, you're gonna make me cry."

"Mark my words—Ryan and Bobby will be engaged by Christmas."

Lily wondered if either of them had met someone special at the dance. Both were a little more private than Andrew, who'd always worn his heart right on the ole sleeve. She had seen her other two brothers talking to a couple different women through the night, so maybe they had. The dance seemed to be magical for all the Hunts.

She recalled watching Andrew dip Heidi during a slow song and kiss her. She'd even snapped a photo, which she'd surprise him with one day. "And what about you?" she asked, wiggling her eyebrows.

She could see his cheeks flush and a big dopey smile light his face. "I've already been looking at rings. Maybe you could help me pick one out? I want to propose on her birthday in October."

"Awww! Andrew! I'm happy for you! And of course I'll help you ring shop!" She gave him a big hug.

Now all she had to do was get her own love life in order. And she had a whole weekend to work on it.

Chapter Thirteen

The Northwest Montana's Best Chef Contest was being held in the Kalispell Luxury Lodge, which was a bit on the outskirts of town. The sprawling one-story guest ranch had an enormous hunter-green peaked roof with the name of the hotel across it. It wasn't as luxe as the Maverick Manor, but there were wide planked floors covered with gorgeous rugs, leather love seats and arm-chairs in sitting areas, and pots of flowers everywhere. On the other side of the hotel reception desk, two women sat at a registration table for the contest. There were at least thirty people in line, mostly in rows of two. The chefs and their assistants.

"Yikes, I hope being in line by the deadline counts," Lily said to Xander. It was only five thirty so she was sure they'd make it to the table by six.

The guy in front of her, wearing a bright purple apron, turned around and said, "It does—I asked!"

"Phew," Lily said. "Thanks."

Xander slung his arm around her, and she felt instantly cheered. They'd chatted nonstop on the way to Kalispell, a forty-five-minute drive, and she wondered if both of them were filling in any potential silences before they could happen. Maybe he'd figured she'd use the time to talk about what had happened between the night of the dance and the next morning. But she was not going to bring that up.

This weekend would speak for itself.

She just had to let it.

He seemed to sense she was a little nervous about what to expect from tonight's elimination round, so while they waited in line he stayed mostly silent, though his arm was a constant comfort around her shoulder.

The line moved quickly, since there were two people handling the check-ins. Finally, Lily was up.

"Hi, I'm Lily Hunt for the competition," she said to the blonde on the left.

As the woman handed her a form to sign, a name tag to fill out and instructions to report to the Sagebrush Ballroom down the hall, someone tapped her on the shoulder.

"Lily!" a male voice said with faux cheer.

She knew that voice.

She turned around. Ugh. It was him. The bane of her existence at the Gold Rush Diner in Rust Creek Falls, where she'd worked for a year as a short-order cook before daring to apply for a line cook job at the Manor. Kyle Kendrick. What a jerk. Luckily, his reputation preceded him because when he tried to get a job at Maverick Manor, her boss, Gwen, had apparently said: "You should watch who you insult while walking down the street. My husband and I were coming toward you and you told him to stop hogging the sidewalk with his 'beer gut.' I almost punched you out myself, but he stopped me."

Kyle was slightly built and not very tall and had a fake-angelic look because of his wavy, light blond hair and blue eyes, which probably saved him from getting beat up as often as he might have. Though she had seen him come to work with a few bruised cheeks.

He was still at the Gold Rush. The only reason he'd lasted there so long was because he was good at his job. Not only good, but fast. She wondered if anyone from the Manor was here for the competition. She hadn't seen any of them, but they might have checked in earlier.

"I plan to win this thing, Hunt," Kyle said, a pretty blonde woman checking her phone beside him. "I want to open a bar and grill focusing on my signature steak-burger. People at the Gold Rush tell me they prefer mine to yours at the Maverick Manor. And for less than a third of the price."

Well whoop-de-do. "I wish you luck," she said. "See you inside." She took Xander's arm, and they headed to the Sagebrush Ballroom. *Please let me be stationed far away from him*, she said in a little prayer.

"My brothers and I had steakburgers the other day at the Gold Rush," Xander said. "And I happened to hear a waitress yelling at someone named Kyle to watch his language, so I know he was there. The steakburger didn't come *close* to yours."

"I knew I liked you," she said with a grin.

She'd almost said *I knew I loved you*. Almost. Thank the universe she'd caught herself.

They entered the Sagebrush Ballroom and got on an-other line, this one much shorter. There were hundreds of chairs, most full, set up at a good distance from several rows of tables where ten people stood making something on what looked like hot plates. Three more people with clipboards were walking among the tables, taking bites of something, then jotting something down on their clipboards.

Oh gosh. This had to be the elimination round. Hot-plate cooking? And what were they making? From the smell of it, could be grilled cheese.

She watched a different man with a clipboard and headphones hand the woman in front of her a number, then direct her to take a seat. Then it was Lily's turn.

"You're number two hundred forty-six," the man said to Lily. He wore a name tag that read Hal. "You can take a seat and wait for the grouping with your number to be called."

Lily's eyes practically bugged out. "Did you say two hundred forty-six? That's a lot of entrants."

"Tell me about it," he said. "Our judges' stomachs are getting seriously full. But the deadline to register here at the hotel just passed, so there shouldn't be too many more of you. Good luck," he added before gesturing for her and Xander to take seats.

"Suddenly I'm not as sure of myself," Lily whispered to Xander. "There could be three hundred people entering, who all think they have what it takes to win."

"Yes, but only you truly do," Xander said, slinging that strong, comforting arm over her shoulder again.

She smiled and shook her head. "I'm glad you're here," she whispered.

"You've got this."

Lately, Lily felt like she could do anything. But when Xander was by her side, she *knew* she could.

"Numbers two forty through two fifty, please appear in a line at the first table. Chefs only—no assistants."

"Gulp. I'm on my own," she said, standing up.

"Like I said, you've got this." He kissed her hand and she almost gasped. "For good luck," he added.

She wouldn't mind a *real* good-luck kiss—on the lips—but she'd settle for the hand. *For now*, she thought with a devilish smile.

She hurried up to the table with the nine others on their way. Ugh again! Kyle Kendrick was right in front of her. Of all the times to arrive, she had to pick the same time he had?

"Hope your grilled cheese doesn't burn," he said, barely turning around.

"Oh, yours, too," she said, rolling her eyes.

Interestingly, while the line formed, staff were scrubbing at the hot plates to get rid of any former cooking residue. At least she wouldn't be dealing with a burned-on mess from her predecessor.

The ten of them were directed to enter the rows of tables and to stand behind the hot plate with their number beside it. Kyle was two forty and the first in his row. Lily was first in her row at the table adjacent.

The man with the clipboard appeared. "Welcome to the elimination round! I'm Hal and your emcee for the competition. Because we have so many entrants, this seemed the best way to narrow down the field to the top ten chefs. Good luck to all of you!"

Lily eyed Xander, who had moved to the front row, close to where she stood. She smiled at him, and he flashed her a thumbs-up.

"You will each make the perfect grilled cheese with the simplest of ingredients," Hal continued. "White bread. American cheese and half a cup of butter. A staffer will now hand out your ingredients."

Next to the hot plate was a butter knife, a plastic spatula and a salad-type plate. A young woman handed Lily a small tray containing two slices of bread, the butter and two slices of yellow American cheese.

Once the ten hopefuls had their ingredients, the man with the clipboard continued. "You have fifteen minutes to make the perfect grilled cheese, which will then be voted on by our three judges. Ready, set, turn on your hot plates!"

Lily pressed the little red on button. She could feel the hot plate warming up.

Hal looked at his watch. "Three, two, one, and begin!"

Lily dropped some butter on the hot plate, then slathered both sides of the bread, every speck, with the remaining butter. Because she couldn't control the temperature of the hot plate the way she could a burner at home, she decided to put one slice of cheese on each piece of bread and start that way. Once the cheese started melting, she flipped one onto the other, gave a gentle press with the spatula, then flipped, then flipped again. When the outside of the bread was golden brown and the cheese looking perfectly gooey, she turned off the hot plate and slid the grilled cheese onto the plate.

"One minute remaining!" the man with the clipboard said.

Lily flipped the sandwich over on the plate, then cut it, hoping she'd timed it right and the cheese was sufficiently gooey in the center. Yes—looked like it was!

She glanced over at Xander, who was at nodding at her with a smile. *Looks Lily Hunt good*, he mouthed, and she grinned.

A judge began on each section of the table. A blonde woman cut a piece of Lily's sandwich, her expression giving nothing away. She took another bite, then jotted down something on her clipboard. The two other judges did the same.

Their group was then dismissed.

Lily rushed over to Xander. "I have no idea how I did. Hot plate grilled cheese isn't exactly my specialty."

"Probably why they chose that method—because the best chefs will know how to make an incredible grilled cheese with very limited resources. And I'm sure yours will be among the top ten."

She dropped down on the chair beside him, watching the next group go. The smell of burning cheese soon filled the air, but the good AC system and fans took care of it. The poor chef responsible started to cry, then shut off her hot plate and stormed off.

"Well, that's one less cook to worry about," Xander whispered. "And who knows how many others stalked off before the results were announced."

Lily fidgeted in her seat for the next half hour, till it was over and Hal announced that the judges would have their results within minutes.

"Gulp," Lily said, grabbing Xander's hand and squeezing it.

He kissed her cheek and she felt so comforted that she just leaned her head against his shoulder.

"Okay, entrants!" Hal called out. "Thank you all for coming and making your grilled cheese for us! We know that all of you are great chefs, but alas, only ten can move on to the next round. And so, in no particular order, here are the names of our final ten contestants!"

Lily squeezed Xander's hand harder.

Hal had named eight chefs so far—five women and three men, including that horrid Kyle Kendrick, who'd let out a "Yeah, baby!"

Please, please, please, she prayed silently. *Pleeeeeze!*

"Our ninth contestant is Lily Hunt."

Lily's mouth dropped open just as Xander pulled her into a hug.

"You did it!" he said, kissing the top of her head. "You rock!"

She barely heard the name of the tenth contestant. All she knew was that Xander's arms were around her and she'd made it into the next round.

Right now, life couldn't get better.

"I'm sorry, but I only see a reservation for Lily Hunt," the woman at the hotel reception desk said. "A single. There's no reservation for Xander Crawford—and we're booked for the competition. There's a hotel two miles away you could try."

Two miles away from Lily? No, Xander thought.

"Surely you have *one* extra room somewhere in the hotel for a hardworking rancher assisting the best chef in Montana," Xander said, turning on the charm. He *could* when it was necessary.

"Northwest, but thank you," Lily said.

Xander put his arm around her shoulder. "All of Montana. The country, probably."

The woman behind the reception desk had an "aww" look on her face, but it didn't seem to help the cause. "Sorry. As I said, we're booked solid. There's just one reservation for your party."

Lily frowned. "But I was told we'd have two single rooms. Adjoining."

"I'm sorry, miss. There's nothing I can do."

"I can check into the other hotel," Xander told Lily. "No biggie."

Lily shook her head. "No way. We'll bunk together."

"You sure?" he asked. Innocently. As if he hadn't been hoping she'd say exactly that. Sharing a room with Lily tonight? Just what he wanted.

Sometimes a guy needed time to think while the object of his confusion was right there.

"Of course." She leaned toward the woman behind the desk. "Please tell me the bed is at least a full size and not a twin?"

"It's a full," she assured her with a smile.

Xander nodded at Lily. "Well, there you go. Room for us both." Except Xander was six foot two and a hundred eighty pounds. He hadn't slept in a full-size bed since middle school.

Once they were registered—and Xander insisted on handing over his credit card—they went to the elevator. Lily was quiet on the ride up, probably a little uncomfortable about sharing a room after all that had happened between them—and not happened—so he held both their bags and let her have her thoughts.

"You're sure you're okay with sharing a room?" he asked as he led the way to a door marked 521. "I can be back and forth in a flash. Two miles is nothing."

The truth? Two miles was forever when it came to being near Lily. He could barely stand being away from her back home.

"It's fine," she said. "We're…whatever we are. I can handle one night. You'll just stay far on your side of the bed."

"Scout's honor," he said, holding up the three-fingered symbol.

Unless neither of them would be able to resist the other and a twin bed would have suited just fine, he thought.

The room was tiny. Barely enough space for the bed, which sure looked small, a dresser with a TV over it, a desk and chair in the corner, and a small bathroom but a jetted tub. He'd definitely take advantage of that.

While Lily unpacked her bag, he opened up the curtains. They did have a view of the mountains. Way off in the distance, but they were majestic and beautiful. He could stare at mountain peaks all day.

"So, what should we do tonight?" she asked. "There's a restaurant in the hotel or we could go explore Kalispell. There are some great restaurants."

"Let's explore," he said.

She smiled. "Just give me five minutes to change."

He was wearing a button-down shirt and his nice jeans, so thought he'd just stay in that. He went over to the full-length mirror on the wall by the bathroom and gave his hair a tousle, smoothed his shirt and then went back over to the window to look at the mountains of Glacier National Park.

"All ready," Lily said, coming out of the bathroom.

He turned toward her and gaped. Holy cannoli.

Humina, humina, humina.

She wore a sleeveless black minidress with a V-neck, a delicate gold necklace dangling in just the hint of cleavage. *Sexy* did not begin to describe how she looked. Her gorgeous red hair was sleek past her shoulders, and her slightly shimmery red lips beckoned him close.

All of a sudden he realized he was standing a foot in front of her. Staring.

"You surprise me constantly," he whispered. "There are so many facets to you and I love them all."

"Do you?" she whispered back.

He'd tripped a bit on the word *love* once it had left his mouth. But he'd meant it and nodded. "You're amazing, Lily Hunt."

She smiled and now it was her eyes that were shimmering. "You always know what to say. It's what I love about *you*."

"Well, I don't say what I don't mean."

She squeezed his hand and then headed for the door as if she needed to escape this conversation, and he understood why. He was confusing. He was confusing her. And he hated that about himself. His words, his actions very clearly said something about how he felt about Lily. But he seemed to be ruled by a very stubborn brain that had called a halt to letting him really feel all that she engendered in him.

They left the hotel and drove to downtown Kalispell, a very different town than Rust Creek Falls. Home barely had five hundred residents. Kalispell around twenty thousand. The streets were bustling with tourists and residents, heading into the many shops and restaurants.

Xander parked in a public lot, and they started toward the main drag. "Thai?" he suggested, pointing across the street. "Italian? Japanese?"

"You know what I'm dying for? Barbecue. Or chili. Something that sticks to your ribs."

"Say no more. My brother Hunter told me about a new American place that has both. Montana Hots, it's called." He did a search on his phone. "Just four blocks up."

She smiled and wrapped her arm around his. "Gorgeous night. It's fun getting out of Rust Creek Falls, though I love it there. All these people and the different shops and eateries. Sure is exciting."

"I agree," he said, opening the door to Montana Hots. The place was pretty big so there wasn't a wait. They decided on a table outside with huge planters of flowers creating a barrier to the next restaurant.

Lily ordered Grandma Cheyenne's Blue-Ribbon Chili. Xander went for the ribs, which came with way too many sides, but he never passed up garlic mashed potatoes and coleslaw.

"I wonder if one day I'll have a place like this," she said once the waitress left. "I always thought I'd have a restaurant of my own. But I'll tell ya, when my client, Mr. Parster, said I should be cooking for the town as a personal chef, something just lit up inside me like a firecracker. I instantly knew that's what I want to do right now. Have my own business, cook to order, develop a clientele. Maybe five years down the road, I'll seriously think about a restaurant."

The waitress returned with their drinks, two spiked lemonades.

"You can definitely count on seven hungry Crawfords being on that client list," he said. "So if I want a rib eye steak and roast potatoes delivered to my home, all I have to do is text you?"

"Yup. I'll do meals on call, but I'm also planning a meal kit business. I provide the ingredients, all wrapped up, and cooking instructions, so there's no shopping or measuring necessary. An easy-to-make meal for two or four or six. I'll have a rotating menu. I'll also have a menu for all dietary plans. Gluten free, vegan, vegetarian, low-carb, you name it. Lily's Home Cookin'. That's what I'm naming my business."

"Lily's Home Cookin'. I could have that every day. And most likely will."

She held up her lemonade with a smile, and he clinked their glasses.

Suddenly he pictured himself sitting at a table in a house, their house, about to gobble up whatever incredible dish his Best Chef in Montana had dreamed up.

Their house.

Sometimes, when he thought of him and Lily that way, in a fantasy way, he didn't get all tied up in knots over the reality. Sometimes, it just felt right.

Their entrées were served, his ribs incredible and Lily's chili, which she held up to his mouth in a big spoonful, equally delicious. They talked about their own grandmas' chili, though in Xander's case, it was Grandpa's chili that everyone in the family lined up for when they got together. They talked about her hopes for Lily's Home Cookin', and then Lily said something that had him practically choking on his garlic mashed potatoes.

"I think in about six months, once my business is in a good groove, I'll be able to focus on my personal life. I've really ignored it for far too long."

He paused, his fork hovering in midair. "Your personal life? What do you mean?"

"Well, my love life. I might be young, Xander, but I'm an old soul. I think, anyway. I'm ready to settle down. Find my guy. The man I'm meant to be with forever."

He swallowed, the dry lump going down hard.

"I may even ask Viv Dalton to set me up." She smiled and took a spoonful of her chili, then tore off some corn bread.

How could she eat at a time like this?

When she was talking about finding a husband. Another man. Not him.

He was not ready to let her go.

But he wasn't ready for anything else, either.

Cripes.

Luckily, she changed the subject to corn bread and how her dad always made it on Sundays. "Even when we all realized I was a really good cook, he still insisted on making the Sunday corn bread the way my mom used to. I love that."

"Is it any good?" Xander asked, then finished off the last rib.

"I love my dad like crazy, but no. It's terrible! I'm not even quite sure what he keeps forgetting. Maybe a different ingredient every time."

He smiled. "Corn bread is like French fries and pizza. Even bad, it's good."

Lily laughed, that sound he loved. And the thought of some other guy hearing that melodic, happy laugh for the rest of his life was like a punch to his gut.

Dinner over, they decided on dessert somewhere else, and found a make-your-own frozen yogurt shop full of customers. Xander made a bizarre pistachio, mocha-chip concoction, with a zillion toppings, while Lily went for the strawberry shortcake fro-yo with multicolored sprinkles. They walked and ate, people watching, window-shopping, oohing and ahhing over cute dogs of all sizes in a pet store display.

And then they were done with their desserts and it was getting late, so they headed back to the hotel since they needed to be in the hotel kitchen at 7:00 a.m. Apparently, the Luxury Lodge had three kitchens, and for the weekend, the competition would be using the small one designed specifically for room service.

Lily was quiet in the elevator up to the fifth floor. Because she was thinking about tomorrow?

Or tonight?

Probably both. He slid the card key into the slot on the door, and they headed inside, his gaze landing on the small bed. They would be sharing that tonight.

"Well, I'll just go change into my pj's," Lily said.

He swallowed. Would her pj's be as sexy as her little black dress?

She dashed into the bathroom with some garments in her hand and her tote bag. A few minutes later she emerged in navy blue gym shorts and a fitted white T-shirt.

Yes, her pj's were as sexy as her black dress.

Her hair was in a topknot, and he could barely take his eyes off her long neck. There were freckles on her neck.

"Your turn," she said, slipping into bed, sliding to the very edge. He was surprised she didn't fall between the bed and the wall.

He grabbed a pair of basketball shorts and a T-shirt, changed in the bathroom and came out to find Lily with the blanket pulled up to her chin. He slid beside her, trying to not brush against her, but the bed was pretty small. Lying next to her without touching her was going to make for a hell of a long, sleepless night.

"Good night," she whispered.

He turned to face her. "Good night. Good luck tomorrow."

She smiled, the slight illumination from the moonlight that spilled in through the filmy section of curtains lighting her beautiful face, the freckles he loved so much. "You're my good-luck charm."

"Glad to be," he said.

She closed her eyes and then turned to face the wall, so he turned to face the windows, knowing he'd get zero sleep.

Chapter Fourteen

Lily must have been so tired and stressed about the competition and about sharing a room with Xander that she'd fallen right asleep. How she'd managed that, she had no idea. But the next time her eyes opened, it was morning, her cell phone alarm buzzing at 5:45 a.m.

Xander was on the floor, bare-chested, doing crunches. Of course he was.

"Morning, sleepyhead," he said. "You're gonna knock 'em dead this morning."

"God, please don't let me poison a judge," she said, her eyes widened.

He smiled. "Lil, it's an expression."

Deep breath, girl, she told herself. "I'm just so nervous. I have to win. I have to."

"You will. Believe it and it shall be so."

She laughed. "Who said that?"

"I forget. Yul Brynner in some movie?"

She cracked up and shook her head. "Last one in the shower is a rotten egg!"

"Are you inviting me to shower with you?" he asked, standing up. All six foot two of him. Bare-chested.

"Absolutely not." Though she'd love it. But no way. She was not letting anything about their not-romance get in the way of making it into the next round.

He grinned. "Go ahead. Ladies first."

She grabbed some stuff from the closet and her tote bag and shut the bathroom door behind her. The hot shower did her worlds of good, soothing her muscles, cramped from trying not to brush up against Hottie when he'd first slid in bed beside her last night.

She got dressed in her new skinny jeans, her lucky red T-shirt with the Daisy's Donuts logo on it, and her trusty clogs, and then took three deep breaths. She dried her hair with the weak blow-dryer on the wall, then emerged to find Xander doing push-ups.

Hot. Hot. Hot. He got up and headed in the bathroom with his clothes, and was out within ten minutes, dressed casually and looking gorgeous.

The lobby offered a continental breakfast for guests, and though Lily could barely eat right now, they stopped there. With a strong cup of hazelnut caffeine in her and half a blueberry muffin, she was good to go when they hit the kitchen at six fifty.

As she and Xander entered the kitchen where the contest would be held all day, there were murmurs that it would be like *The Great British Baking Show*, where they'd be given the ingredients and a recipe, and would have to make the same thing.

"You're all going down," Kyle Kendrick said with a toss of his blond bangs.

"In your dreams, blondie," a woman with very long dark hair said.

Hal, the emcee with the ever-present clipboard, came in. "Okay, contestants and assistants. Each of you was given a number when you entered the kitchen. Please stand at the station that has your number on the cupboard."

Lily was number five—which had always been one of her favorite numbers. Her birthday was on the fifteenth. And she'd been hired at the Maverick Manor on May 25 of the previous year. Lots of good fives in her life.

She'd met Xander on August 6, but it was close.

The kitchen had ten stations, each with its own four-burner stove, oven, stainless steel counter space, mini fridge, sink and cupboards. She and Xander stood at the counter, which faced the front of the kitchen, where Hal stood with his clipboard and headset.

"This morning, you will make a perfect Western omelet. Seven of you will be eliminated. Three of you will move on to the final round this afternoon. In the drawer of your counter you will find a recipe for the omelet. You will find all the ingredients and utensils you need in your station, along with a full spice rack. You will have twenty minutes to make your perfect Western omelet. Oh—and I will answer your burning question: yes, you may alter the recipe to suit yourself. Of course, that may get you in trouble or it may put you in the lead. Who knows?" he added with a devilish grin. "Assistants, you may take one minute to familiarize yourself with the cupboards while the cooks peruse the recipe. Ready, set, go!"

While Lily pulled open the drawer and took out

the recipe, Xander opened the cupboards and the mini fridge. The recipe was basic. She'd definitely enhance it. This was about being the best—not being safe.

This morning at the continental breakfast buffet, she happened to overhear two of the contestants talking about the judges. Two were married and from New Orleans originally; they'd gotten married there on a Mississippi riverboat cruise, which made her think they probably had good associations with their hometown. Perhaps a little taste of home in her Western omelet would give her a slight edge with them, and be just delicious enough to sway the third judge. Lily had no idea where he was from.

"Contestants! You have twenty minutes. Starting in... three, two, one, cook!"

"Okay, what do you need?" Xander asked her.

"I need a medium sauté pan and a spatula. I'll grab the ingredients."

In moments, the right pan and the perfect spatula were on the counter. Lily got the burner to the right level, added butter to the pan and began beating five eggs. She added a small amount of milk, then beat the mixture some more.

"Xander, I need you to finely dice one onion, one green pepper and one yellow pepper. Put all your love for beautiful vegetables into your work. Meanwhile, I'll dice the ham."

"Got it!" Xander said, rushing to the pantry. "All my love for onion and peppers coming up." He pulled out the ingredients, got out a chopping board and began dicing away. "Love you, onion that I'm cutting with a really sharp knife. Chop, chop, chop."

"Um, could you keep it down over there?" snapped

the guy at the station to their left. He was in his forties and wore a neon-green apron that said I Can Explain It to You but I Can't Understand It for You. How nice. "I'm trying to concentrate."

"I can talk *and* concentrate," Xander told him. "But I'll try to lower my voice."

"Gee, thanks," the guy said.

Lily smiled at Xander and rolled her eyes, then continued dicing the ham. She added it to the pan, giving it a stir.

"Done," Xander said, bringing over his chopping board.

He slid the very nicely diced vegetables in the pan, and Lily sautéed them in the butter, waiting until they softened. Hmm, the onions and peppers and ham smelled heavenly. Of course, the entire kitchen smelled amazing.

"You stupid buffoon!" the woman at the station to the right of Lily screamed. At her assistant—who was red in the face. "How could you drop the eggs? We only had five!" The woman turned to Hal with the clipboard. "Hal, I can get more eggs, right? My idiot sister dropped ours and they're all over the floor."

"Sorry," Hal said. "No more eggs in your fridge, no omelet, so that disqualifies you. Please pack up and leave the kitchen. You are *not* Northwest Montana's Best Chef."

The woman was seething. "And this is not *Top Chef*!" she yelled, then stalked off, her poor sister trailing.

"Sorry," the sister said meekly, and ran off after the former contestant.

"Ooh, that's too bad," Xander said. "Thanksgiving sure won't be fun for them this year."

"Right?" Lily said, shaking her head.

"And then there were nine!" Kyle Kendrick called out.

Jerk.

"Ten minutes, Lil," Xander said.

She nodded and flashed him a thumbs-up, then Lily added the eggs to the pan, debating whether to add a little cheese. There were four kinds in the fridge, but a true Western omelet, a purist one, didn't have cheese. She'd skip it.

"Four minutes, Lily," Xander said.

"Four minutes left!" the assistant behind their station bellowed.

"Oh hell!" someone shouted. "The omelet's stuck to the pan!"

"I am so gonna win," said Kyle Kendrick. "No one makes an omelet like I do. No to the one!"

"Yes, chef!" his assistant said. She happened to be the pretty blonde Lily had seen draped over Kyle last night in the lobby as she and Xander returned from Kalispell.

Lily rolled her eyes so hard that Xander cracked up.

"Find that funny, do you?" Kyle said, glaring at him. "You'll see."

Now it was Xander's turn to roll his eyes.

"Eyes on your own paper, kids," Xander whispered.

Lily laughed and high-fived him.

"Two minutes, chef!" Kyle's blonde said.

"Two minutes, Lil," Xander said, getting a glare from Kyle.

She loved that he was having a good time. Competitions could seriously stress out some people, but Xander rolled with it, doing a very careful and good job.

Just before she flipped the omelet she added a hint of tabasco sauce and a dash of cayenne pepper across the omelet to bring that little taste of New Orleans. The omelet looked absolutely divine, if she did say so herself.

"Can I eat that?" Xander asked.

"If there's any left over," she said, giving her shoulders a shimmy. She waited until the bottom of the omelet was the perfect shade, then flipped the sides onto each other.

Done.

She plated, added a sprinkle of kosher salt and a little pepper—and waited.

"Time!" Hal called. "The judges will now begin their rounds. Please provide three forks."

Xander handed Lily three forks, which she placed on three folded napkins next to the plates.

The female judge came over and studied the omelet and then made some notations. She took a bite, then another, looked at Lily, and made a notation, then moved on.

When her husband, one of the two male judges, took a bite, Lily swore he closed his eyes with a tiny sigh, but that might have been her fantasy. He made his notes. The third judge took three bites, always a good sign, and jotted his comments.

"My goodness!" said the female judge to a contestant two rows behind Lily. "How much salt did you add?"

Lily heard crying. She felt so sorry for whichever contestant it was that she didn't even turn around. Xander didn't, either. He just squeezed her hand.

"That's two down!" Kyle announced. "Eight of us left."

"Jerk," Xander whispered.

After conferring with the three judges, Hal stepped forward. "And the three contestants moving into round two are…"

Lily held her breath.

* * *

Xander tried to remember the last time he'd prayed. When he was a kid, around four or five. He'd wait at the window for his mother to come back, but she never did. So he started praying every night, since someone at school had told him that was how you got stuff you wanted.

His mother had never come back.

He prayed now—to the universe, to nature, to the big man upstairs. *Let Lily's name be called, please!*

"Kyle Kendrick!" Hal announced.

Crud, Xander thought.

"Boo-yah!" Kyle said, fist-pumping his way up and down the aisle. "Where do the winners stand?" he asked.

"You can stay at your station for now," Hal said. With the teensiest note of disdain, unless that was wishful thinking. Probably was.

"Kerry Atalini!" Hal called next.

There were six contestants left. Xander took Lily's hand and held it, and he wondered if she could feel him praying beside her. He was thinking that hard.

She closed her eyes, too.

"And our third and final contestant moving on to the final round—Lily Hunt!"

Her eyes popped open. Xander picked her up and whirled her around, then kissed her solidly on the mouth.

"You did it!" Xander whispered in her ear. "And this afternoon, you will beat both other contestants and win the ten grand!"

She threw her arms around him and hugged him and he held her tight. He was so proud of her. So proud *for* her.

"Contestants, we will reconvene at noon on the dot

in this kitchen for the final round. Only one of you will be named Northwest Montana's Best Chef!"

"Sorry, Lily, but it's going to be *me*," Kyle said, sauntering by her with his assistant trailing him on her high heels. How she puttered around the station in those three-inch things was beyond him.

Xander ignored him. "Any idea what the final-round meal is?" he asked Lily as they left the kitchen and headed for the elevator.

"No clue. But I feel ready for anything. Thank you so much for being a great assistant, Xander."

"You taught me everything I know," he said, batting his eyes.

She gave him a playful sock on the arm. "Seriously. Thank you."

"You are very welcome."

The moment they got into the room, Lily said she wanted to take another shower and get the smell of peppers and onions out of her hair and skin. When he heard the water turn on, he wished he was in that shower stall with her. Washing her beautiful body. Lathering up her hair. Making soapy love to her.

He parked himself on the desk chair, his attention on the bathroom door. On the water running. He had Lily on the brain. Every part of him craved her, wanted her.

The water stopped. The bathroom door opened. Lily came out, her hair damp, her body wrapped in a small white towel.

She stared at him as she walked over, then straddled him on the chair.

Ooh boy.

Hadn't he said she was full of surprises?

"One of us has too many clothes on," she whispered.

"Yeah, *you*." He slowly undid the towel, reveling in every gorgeous naked bit of her.

She undid his belt buckle. Then the snap of his jeans. The zipper came down. He picked her up in his arms and carried her to the bed, grabbing a condom from his wallet—he always kept one in there, but he'd brought five for this weekend. Wishful thinking. And good thing he had.

Then they were under the covers, a tangle of arms and legs and hungry lips.

Once again, she rocked his world. That was no longer a surprise.

"I love you," she whispered as she climaxed, and Xander froze. Just for a second.

But Lily must have felt it because she pulled back a bit, looking at him. "I shouldn't have said that. I didn't mean to say it—it just burst out of my mouth."

"Lily, I…"

"Oh, that again," she said, the look of disappointment so pronounced that he tried to force the words but they still wouldn't come.

Did he love her? All signs pointed to yes, but then why couldn't he say so? Why couldn't he even say so to himself?

He heard her sigh. "I should really be focusing on the next round," she said. "I'd better get dressed and go in search of some strong coffee. I don't know what came over me, why I jumped your bones. Let's forget the whole thing. I'm just running on competition adrenaline. This. Never. Happened." He'd come to know her so well that he could see she was hiding her misery behind a plastered-on fake smile.

"Lily, I—"

But she'd grabbed some clothes from the closet and shut herself in the bathroom.

When she emerged, he was dressed, too, and hoping they could talk, but again, he was tongue-tied. Stuck, really. That was how he felt: stuck. In what, by what, he wasn't sure.

"I'll see you at eleven fifty in the kitchen," she said, grabbed her tote bag and rushed out of the room.

Xander might not know if he loved her, but he sure felt like he hated himself at that moment.

Lily sat in the lobby, sipping her second excellent cappuccino, trying not to think of the humiliation she'd just endured.

I love you.

I...don't. Sorry.

Fine, he hadn't said that. But the "Lily, I..." followed by nothing said as much.

She knew this already. Why had she jumped his bones? Why had she blurted out the true depth of her feelings for him?

Because you love him. And you're not hiding anymore. This is me. I'm a passionate person who loves hard and if I feel it, I'm gonna express it.

Tears stung her eyes and she blinked them back.

She'd tried to be so tough last night, telling him she was looking forward to finding her guy and settling down soon. She'd been hoping to make him realize she wasn't going to be around forever, that some other man would snap her right up.

But he hadn't even reacted. And so she'd changed the subject and tried to move on from thinking about romance to just focusing on the contest.

But the high of making it to the final round was so profound that she'd felt like Wonder Woman for a while there, floating up to their room in a haze of happiness and pride. She'd been named a finalist with Xander beside her, Xander helping her. That made it all the more sweet.

And in the shower, all she could think of was how badly she wanted him in there with her. She'd planned her little daylight seduction right then and there. And she went for it.

So had he.

Until she'd come out with the *I love you*.

Cripes.

"Hi, Lily!" said a female voice.

It was Kerry, the other contestant besides Kyle in the final round. Kerry was in her late twenties or early thirties with dark pixie-cut hair and black framed eyeglasses. She had a tattoo of a pink cupcake on her shoulder. Lily recalled that her assistant was a woman who looked a lot like her, her sister probably. "How amazing is this?" Kerry said. "Almost three hundred entrants, and it's down to three of us. I can't even believe it."

"I know. I can't, either. I came here hoping and praying but not expecting."

Kerry smiled. "Ditto. Although I think what's-his-name expects to win."

"Ugh," Lily said. "He's from my hometown. He's good but he's not exactly the nicest guy."

"Well, then I hope it's one of us. Ladies unite!" she said with a grin. "What do you plan to do with the money if you win?"

Lily explained about Lily's Home Cookin' and hoping to get that business off the ground without having to take out a loan.

"What a great idea!" Kerry said. "I love it. I live an hour from here in the opposite direction or I'd definitely order me some Lily's Home Cookin'."

Lily grinned. Kerry was a sweetheart. "So how about you? What are your plans?"

"I really want to open a small casual café where moms can bring their kids and the little ones can run around. I'll have a train set on a table, and dolls and trucks and Legos and blocks. A reading nook. I love to cook but my real love is baking, so I'll have amazing pastries and maybe offer some light kid fare, like grilled cheese. I know I do that really well."

Lily laughed, recalling their elimination round entrée. "Right? Do you have a child?"

"Samantha," Kerry said, a wistful look coming over her face. "She's two and a half and the love of my life. Her dad took off on me, but left me with the best part of himself, so hey, I'm happy. My mom's watching her for me while I'm here."

"Aww, that's really great. My assistant is the love of my life but he just thinks of me as a friend."

Kerry gave Lily a "you're crazy" expression. "Uh, I saw with my own eyes how that incredibly hot guy looks at you, talks to you and acts around you. He's a man in love. Trust me."

Sarah seemed to think so, too. Why was Xander the only one who didn't see it? "Well, he doesn't want to be, unfortunately."

"Ah, good thing is that you can't stop progress. He'll come around." She glanced at her watch. "It's eleven thirty. I'm gonna go freshen up for the big moment."

Can't stop progress. Hadn't Lily herself said that recently?

"See you soon," Lily said. "Thank you, Kerry. And good luck."

"To you, too, sweetie," Kerry said.

Lily finished her cappuccino, staring out the window, wondering if it could be true, that you really *couldn't* stop progress. Thing was, *was* there progress with Xander when he kept taking a giant step backward?

Sigh.

The final round was a chili cook-off.

Lily seemed really excited about that, all signs of her earlier distress gone. She had a smile on her face and fierce concentration in her eyes, and Xander knew she was full speed ahead on winning this thing.

That was just one of the things he loved about her. Her determination. Her drive. She might be hurting, but she was going to be named Northwest Montana's Best Chef.

"You've got this," he said, squeezing her hand at their station. He wanted to ask if she was okay, if they were good, but this wasn't the time to talk about them. They had to concentrate on the contest.

"Let's do it!" she said, those beautiful green eyes flashing with spirit.

I love you, too, he thought. And almost said it right there.

I love you, Lily Hunt. I flipping love you!

Holy hell. He loved her!

Minutes later, he had to table that incredible revelation to focus on being Lily's assistant. He chopped and diced, he handed over the packages of meat and beans, he found the right pots and pans and utensils.

Kyle Kendrick boasted up a storm at the station in the middle, snapping at his assistant, who Xander hoped would tell him to shove it and walk out on him. But unfortunately, she kept taking his unnecessary criticism. Hopefully, she'd get sick of it soon enough.

"Ow!" shrieked the woman on the far right station. Kerry, her name was. "Burned myself a bit."

"You okay, Ker?" Lily called over.

"I'll live!" Kerry called back.

"Can I concentrate here? Jeez," Kyle complained.

"Oh, shut it, Kyle," Kerry announced with glee. Her assistant, also with short dark hair, clapped. Xander almost clapped, too. Kerry's assistant wrapped the burn in a Band-Aid, and Kerry was on the move again, dashing between stirring pots and pans.

Finally, time was up. Lily's chili smelled amazing. Looked amazing. Tasted amazing. She had to win this. She *had* to.

The three judges took their bites. Made their notations.

Hal appeared again in the front of the stations, the three judges beside him, ready to announce the results. "In third place, Kyle Kendrick!" Hal announced.

Kyle's mouth dropped open. "There has to be a mistake. *Third?* No."

"Third," Hal said, consulting his clipboard. Kyle glared at him and stared at the judges. They each nodded.

"This blows. I'm outta here," Kyle said. He stalked off, leaving his assistant just standing there.

"You deserve better," Xander said to her.

The blonde shrugged and sighed and went racing after Kyle.

"In second place…" Hal began.

Xander held his breath. He grabbed Lily's hand and squeezed, hoping he wasn't cutting off her circulation.

"Lily Hunt!" Hal continued.

What? There has to be some mistake. Second? No.

Jeez. Now he knew how Kyle felt.

He looked at Lily, who attempted a smile. "Hey, I tried, right? Second out of almost three hundred is pretty darn good, right?"

"And our winner, Northwest Montana's Best Chef, is…Kerry Atalini!" Hal said.

The judges began clapping. So did Lily. In fact, she ran over to Kerry and gave her a big hug.

"Congrats, Kerry. I can't wait to visit your café and eat an amazing chocolate croissant while I watch the little ones play trains," Lily said.

Kerry hugged her back. "Thank you, Lily. Can we keep in touch?" They exchanged email addresses and cell phone numbers, and then Lily was back over at their station.

Kerry was presented with her check for ten thousand, and Xander could feel the absolute wistfulness coming off Lily.

"I wish you'd won," he said. "You're the best chef in the world."

Lily squeezed his hand. "At least Kyle didn't win."

"True."

"Let's go home," she said. "I need home."

He nodded, and they thanked Hal and the judges, then left the kitchen and headed to the elevator.

When the door of their room shut behind them, Xander planned to grab Lily in his arms and tell her he loved her, that he'd been bursting with it ever since the start of the chili cook-off. But as she packed her things, the words wouldn't come again. They were stuck behind something.

What the hell? he wondered. *Tell her. Say it!*

If he said *Lily, I...* and couldn't get anything out beyond that, she'd have every right to punch him in the stomach.

"Ready?" she asked, overnight bag slung over her shoulder.

"You okay?"

She nodded. "I really am. I'll apply for a loan on Monday morning. There's a chance I'll get it. Of course, the bank may say I'm too young and untried and don't have enough work history under my belt. But I have a solid business plan. So we'll see."

"I'll front you the money, Lily. I believe in you and I'd be honored to invest in your business. You can pay me back in French dips, filet mignon in garlic butter and cooking lessons."

Her mouth dropped open. "You're going to just give me ten thousand dollars?"

"Yes. I am. For the reasons I just stated."

And because I love you.

But again, the words wouldn't come.

"That's incredibly generous of you," she said. "*Beyond* generous. That you believe in me means the world to me, Xander. But I can't—and won't—take your money. I might be the Rust Creek Falls Cinderella with my makeover, and I definitely believe in Prince Charming, but I'm no princess and I plan to rescue myself. Know what I mean?"

He stared at her, speechless for the moment, but not surprised.

This is why I love you.

So why couldn't he say it?

Chapter Fifteen

On Tuesday afternoon, Xander was in the barn, doing his favorite chore—cleaning out the stalls—when his mind was full of its own muck. He hadn't spoken to Lily since Saturday night, when they'd returned from Kalispell. The ride home had been on the quiet side; Lily had been clearly tired, and they hadn't talked about *them*. Or the most memorable experience he'd ever had in a chair.

He closed his eyes, remembering. Lily in that tiny white towel. Straddling him.

I'm no princess and I plan to rescue myself...

"Hey, Xander," a male voice said.

His brother Knox. "Ran into Lily in town coming out of the bank this morning. I don't think I've ever actually seen someone kick up their heels, but she truly did. I asked her if she won the lottery and just deposited it or something, but apparently she applied for a business loan yesterday and was approved today."

He grinned. Go, Lily. Yeah!

"She's starting her own personal chef and home-cooking kit business," Xander said. "Was I that focused at twenty-three?" He shook his head, full of admiration for Lily.

"Your plan at twenty-three was to date as many pretty women as possible," Knox reminded him. "So no. You were not."

Xander laughed. "Yeah, I guess so. I kept underestimating Lily because of her age. Do you know that because she didn't win the ten grand in the cooking contest, I offered her the money myself and she turned it down? Said she'd rather get a loan and take care of herself."

"She's awesome. No way around it."

Xander nodded, leaning on the rake. "I kept thinking she was too young for me. But maybe I was just using it as an excuse."

Knox rolled his eyes. "Duh. Of course you were. You got burned in Dallas and understandably wanted nothing to do with falling in love again. I get it. But then you *did* fall in love again. And you can't handle it so you're costing yourself the best thing that will ever happen to you. The woman you *love*."

Xander stared at his brother. Knox was always on the intense side, but he was talking straight from the heart right now. "I do love her. I really do."

"So go get her. *If* she'll have you."

You can't live in the past, she'd said.

I plan to rescue myself, she'd said.

What she'd done was rescue him. From *himself*.

He loved her. With all his stupid, guarded heart, which

now felt stretched open wide. He tried to think about Britney and Chase, smiling their fool faces off at the carnival. But all he pictured in his mind was a pair of flashing green eyes, those freckles and that glorious red hair. He tried to picture his mother in her yellow apron and himself waiting by the window. Again, all he saw was Lily, stirring that pot of chili, adding the green chilies and the extra cayenne pepper to infuse the food with home.

To him, Lily meant home. She *was* home.

Knox grabbed the rake out of his hand. "Almighty Lord, Xander. Go. Run."

"I have a stop to make first," he said, heading out of the barn. At the door, he turned back. "Knox?"

"No more excuses. Go!"

"No more excuses," Xander said. "I just wanted to say…thank you."

The ever-serious Knox Crawford nodded, then broke into a smile.

Cloud nine would be a lot better if Xander were up here with her, but she was so dang happy she found herself skipping from room to room of her house.

I got the loan, I got the loan, I got the loan! Lily's Home Cookin' is coming your way, Rust Creek Falls, so watch out! Or better yet, get yer bellies ready!

She turned on the radio on the kitchen counter, swaying to her favorite country station while putting together her very first Lily's Home Cookin' kit. She'd run into Viv Dalton in Daisy's Donuts when she'd taken herself for a celebratory iced mocha latte and had told her all about the loan and her new business. Viv had been so excited for her and said she'd put in an order right then. A home kit for beef bourguignon. Viv's husband loved the intensive, time-consuming dish, but they were both so busy right now, and if they could make the meal together without having to shop and prep for it, that would be ideal.

Exactly what Lily hoped many, many, many residents of Rust Creek Falls would think about her service. Lily had almost walked right into Xander's brother Knox on her way out of the bank this morning, and he said he and his family would keep her in business for years.

Which made her wonder. How was she going to see Xander every day, maybe—very likely, actually—as a customer, and not go crazy?

Stop thinking about him! she yelled at herself. Focus on the beef bourguignon. She had her little containers all ready to go—the chunks of succulent beef, the bacon, the chopped, sliced and diced vegetables, even the flour and oil. As she snapped the lid on the last container, the tomato paste, she couldn't wait to sketch designs for her own labels.

She packed up her cooler bag, included the red wine necessary to make the beef bourguignon, and added a bottle of champagne that Lily had gotten as a gift from one of her clients so that Viv and her husband could celebrate with their meal. She thought about what Viv had said earlier, that she shouldn't really be ordering something so fancy when business was so— But then she'd stopped talking and looked distracted and uncomfortable, and Lily realized that Viv's wedding planning business, which she operated with her friend Caroline Clifton, might be in financial trouble or having some setbacks.

Huh. Maybe that was why Viv had been so quick to agree to a million-dollar payout from Max Crawford if she married off all six Crawford brothers! Not that any-one wouldn't take that deal, but Viv had sure run with it and now the whirlwind of dates made total sense. Viv needed that money.

If this Rust Creek Falls Cinderella had a fairy god-mother, the closest to it would be Vivienne Dalton her-self. After all, it was Viv who'd suggested Lily throw herself into the dating pool for a Crawford. Viv who'd arranged the date with Knox. Which led to her date with Xander in the park.

Tears stung her eyes even though she was smiling at how Viv had believed in her ability to hook a gorgeous Crawford when she'd been a tomboy with tomato sauce on her shirt and flour-stained baggy jeans.

I owe you, Viv, she thought, reaching into her wallet for Viv's check and ripping it up. Lily grabbed her phone and sent Viv a text.

I'm dropping off your beef bourguignon kit in ten min-utes, as discussed. Oh, and I ripped up your check—this special meal from Lily's Home Cookin' is on me. You're my first official client!

Wow, really? Thanks! Viv texted back.

No, thank you, Viv, Lily thought with a smile. *I might not have ended up with love, but thanks to you, I found it.*

With ten minutes to kill, Lily eyed the *Rust Creek Falls Gazette* on the kitchen table and sat down to poke through it. Ooh, she could check apartment listings! She turned to the Apartment and Condos for Rent section, glancing through a few possibilities. But there was a small house for rent, zoned for business and residen-

tial use, right in the center of town off North Broomtail Road.

It was a little out of her price range, but she could cut
back in other areas. She'd hang out her shingle, and have
her customers come to her for meal kits or to place catering orders. With her loan, she could renovate the kitchen
to her specifications, but considering she wouldn't have
four hungry Hunts constantly in the kitchen and eating
up her good ingredients and leftovers, she might not even
need such a huge work space. She circled the ad for the
house, then grabbed her phone, pressing in the telephone
number for the real estate agent.

But the doorbell rang then, so she put the phone down
and got up to answer it.

Xander. In a suit and tie and a Stetson.

He took off the hat and held it against his chest. "Lily,
I have so much to say to you."

She tilted her head and waited. "I'm listening."

"I didn't come to Rust Creek Falls expecting to fall
for anyone. You know I've been burned before."

*Please don't be here to apologize for not loving me.
I couldn't take that.*

"But then out of nowhere," he continued, his dark eyes
intense on hers, "a smart, focused, talented, passionate,
honest, funny, dachshund-loving, hoodie-wearing gorgeous redhead with sparkling green eyes captured my
heart before I even knew she had it in her possession."

Lily gasped and her knees wobbled. She could barely
breathe—or speak.

"I didn't think anything scared me, Lily. But all this
time, I've been so damned afraid of how I feel about you.
And you know what?"

"What?" she managed to whisper.

"You taught me a lot about courage. And let's face it, I just love you too much to let you go."

He loved her!

"Lily, I want to start over with you. Can we?"

She couldn't speak. She couldn't move.

Finally she found her voice. "Nope, we can't start over. But we can pick up where we left off," she added with a grin. "So where were we?"

"On a chair. Naked. In a Kalispell hotel room."

"Maybe we can go back this weekend," she said. "And re-create that moment—changing what happens next."

"Done," he said. "I do want to change what happens next. But now. Not a minute later." He got down on one knee, opening up a black velvet box. A beautiful diamond ring glittered. "Lily Hunt, will you make me the happiest guy alive by becoming my wife?"

"Yes!" she screamed at the top of her lungs.

He stood up and slid the ring on her finger, then picked her up and whirled her around, smothering her with kisses.

"Yes," he repeated. "Forever."

"Forever," she said.

They delivered Viv's beef bourguignon—and the big news that Viv was two down, four to go on the Crawford bachelors. Lily held up her left hand, the emerald-cut diamond, surrounded by diamond baguettes on a gold band, twinkling.

Viv yelled so loudly her husband came running. The four of them cracked open the champagne Lily had brought, then she and Xander left them to make their romantic meal for two. With leftovers, of course.

Then Xander suggested they book a room at the Maverick Manor for a little privacy, so after surprising the heck out of their families with their big news—Knox wasn't the least bit surprised—he booked the honeymoon suite at the Manor.

More champagne. Chocolate-covered strawberries.

And the love of her life, her fiancé, her soon-to-be husband, beside her in the enormous four-poster bed.

Xander held up a chocolate-covered strawberry and dangled it in front of her mouth. "Want to know a secret? The first night I met you, I went home and thought of feeding you strawberries. Now here I am doing it."

"Ha! I knew you liked me from that first not-a-date." She accepted half the strawberry while he ate the other half, then their lips met in a kiss.

"We'll live happily—and hungrily—ever after," she said.

He kissed her again, wrapping her in his arms. "You know that little house you mentioned you saw in the paper?" he asked. "What do you think of us buying our own ranch close to town and I'll build you your own cooking studio and make you the Lily's Home Cookin' sign for it? State-of-the-art kitchen, display cases, reception counter, waiting area—the works."

"Told you I believed in Prince Charming. Here he is," she said with a smile, then burst into tears.

"I hope those are happy tears," he said.

"My cup runneth over, Xander. Thank you. Yes, yes, yes, a million times yes. Maybe while you're at it, you can build a doghouse for Dobby and Harry."

"Definitely," he said. "I love those furry little beasts."

"And I love you."

He kissed her, and they lay together for a moment. "Oh, I just remembered I brought something with me I wanted to show you." He reached into his overnight bag and pulled out an old jewel-encrusted book.

"It's that diary you and your brothers found in your bedroom!" she said, sitting up.

"Yup. I jimmied it open with a screwdriver. I figure it's the only way to find out who it belongs to so that I can try to get it back to its owner."

"Any clues?"

He opened it up to a middle page, and Lily leaned closer to glance at the yellowed pages. "I read through some of it and whoever kept this diary was seriously in love. He or she was involved in a passionate love affair with someone referred to as only 'W.'"

"Ooh, that looks like a love poem," she said, pointing to the right-hand page.

"'My fair W,'" Xander read, "'I cannot stop thinking of you, dreaming of you, wishing we were together. Soon, I hope. Forever yours.'"

"Aww," Lily said. "So romantic!"

He smiled. "I'll go through it and see if I can find some names. It's probably someone from the Abernathy family, so if I come across a first name, maybe someone with history here in town will recognize it."

"Are you going to write me a love poem?" she asked, kissing the side of his neck.

"I'm not much of a writer, but I promise to cherish you just as much as our surprise diary writer cherished the fair W."

"Me, too," she said, and they snuggled in to start the diary from the beginning.

Epilogue

A week later, Lily, in a white satin wedding gown she'd found in a Kalispell bridal boutique and had altered in record time, walked down a red carpet aisle in the Rust Creek Falls Community Center on the arm of her father, who was crying the entire way. She and Xander had chosen this venue over the swanky Maverick Manor because the center could hold the entire town—and the entire town had been invited to their wedding. Between the Hunts going back generations in Rust Creek Falls, and the Crawfords becoming famous for the million-dollar wager on their bachelorhood, everyone wanted to come. The more, the merrier.

Lily now stood with her gorgeous tuxedo-clad groom in front of the minister, so happy she thought she might burst. Xander's brothers were his groomsmen, and his father his best man. Lily's matron of honor was Sarah, and five of her dear friends who'd scattered after high school had come back for the wedding, even on short notice, all managing to find a pale pink dress and silver shoes.

She thought of herself in that pale pink dress and silver ballet flats at the Summer Sunset Dance the night she and Xander had made love for the first time. To her, that color scheme would always represent new beginnings. So she'd chosen it for her bridal party.

In a rush of words and with shimmering eyes, they were pronounced husband and wife, and Xander kissed her so passionately that there wolf whistles, and she even heard Dobby and Harry, guests of course, giving two short barks each.

The reception was held outside under a beautiful open-air tent. Lily had called for a potluck, and everyone had brought something. Food equaled love, and Lily wanted everyone's love at the wedding.

After the first dance, Max Crawford asked to give a toast, and spoke for quite a while about how love kept surprising him. First, Logan had found it with Sarah. Then Xander with Lily. "Watch out, Knox, Hunter, Finn and Wilder. It's gonna come at you hard when you least expect it, with the woman you least expect it with." He winked at Viv, who smiled back, then they all raised their glasses and drank to true love. Surprising love.

Lily smiled at Viv, too. If her wedding planning business was in trouble, at least Lily had helped by taking down one more Crawford brother—and hiring Viv to plan this shindig.

Everyone was crowding around the buffet tables, where champagne and heaps of food waited for the guests. Lily had decided to make her own chili—not the recipe that hadn't won her the cooking contest, but her mother's recipe, a chili to die for. She'd added a little of everything under the sun so that as many people as possible would be reminded of home.

"Brings me back to Texas," Xander said after taking a bite. "There go those crazy memories again. Hunter putting a frog down my shirt. Me beating Logan for the first time in a race." A look of surprise crossed his face. "Hey—strangest thing," he said. "The next memory that flashed at me was you in your T-shirt and jeans, a hoodie wrapped around your waist in the doorway of the Maverick Manor kitchen."

Lily gasped. "That was here. In Montana. The night you showed up as my date."

"Because *this* is home now. Home is always going to be where you are, Lily Crawford."

There were clinks on glasses, which meant the new husband had to kiss his new bride. Under the Big Sky Country's brilliant late-August sun, Xander dipped Lily for the kiss of all kisses, and Lily knew they had indeed found home in each other forever.

* * * * *

Look for the next book in the new
Harlequin Special Edition continuity
Montana Mavericks:
Six Brides for Six Brothers

The Maverick's Wedding Wager
by Joanna Sims

On sale September 2019,
wherever Harlequin books and ebooks are sold.

"Why are you armed with pepper spray? Did something
happen to you?"

She didn't look up.

"Yes. Something happened."

"Here?"

She shook her head, her body trembling so badly
she didn't trust her voice. The only sound was Nick's
wheezing breath. He finally cleared his throat.

"Okay. Something happened." His voice was gravelly
from the pepper spray, but it was calmer than it had been
a few minutes ago. "And you wanted to protect yourself.
That's smart. But you need to do it right. I'll teach you."

Her head snapped up. He was doing his best to look at her, even though his left eye was still closed.

"What are you talking about?"

"I'll teach you self-defense, Cassie. The kind that actually works."

"Are you talking karate or something? I thought the pepper spray…"

"It's a tool, but you need more than that. If some guy's amped up on drugs, he'll just be temporarily blinded and really ticked off." He picked up the pepper spray canister from the grass at her side. "This stuff will spray up to ten feet away. You never should have let me get so close before using it."

"I didn't know that."

"Exactly." He grimaced and swore again. "I need to get home and dunk my face in a bowl full of ice water." He stood and reached a hand down to help her up. She hesitated, then took it.

Don't miss
A Man You Can Trust *by Jo McNally,*
available September 2019 wherever
Harlequin® Special Edition books and ebooks are sold.

www.Harlequin.com

Looking for more satisfying love stories
with community and family at their core?

Check out **Harlequin® Special Edition**
and **Love Inspired®** books!

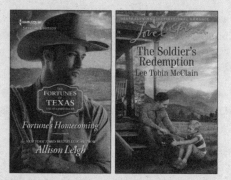

New books available every month!

CONNECT WITH US AT:

Facebook.com/groups/HarlequinConnection

 Facebook.com/HarlequinBooks

Twitter.com/HarlequinBooks

Instagram.com/HarlequinBooks

Pinterest.com/HarlequinBooks

ReaderService.com

**ROMANCE WHEN
YOU NEED IT**

HFGENRE2018

SPECIAL EXCERPT FROM

Meg tensed from head to toe, sucking in her breath as she saw two masculine hands close over the shutters' edges on either side of her body. Then instinctively turned her head to take in light hair, a strong stubbled jaw and blue eyes—no more than an inch from hers.

"I... I..." He smelled good. Not sweaty at all, the way she surely did. The firm muscles in his arms bracketed her shoulders.

"I think I got it if you just wanna kinda duck down under my arm." Despite the awkward situation and the weight of the shutter, the suggestion came out sounding entirely good-natured.

And okay, yes, separating their bodies was an excellent idea. Because she wasn't accustomed to being pressed up against any other guy besides Zack, for any reason, not even practical ones. And a stranger to boot. Who on earth was this guy, and how had he just magically materialized in her yard?

The ducking-under-his-arm part kept her feeling just as awkward as the rest of the contact until it was accomplished. And when she finally freed herself, her rescuer calmly competently lowered the loose shutter to the ground, leaning it against the house with an easy "There we go."

He wore a snug black T-shirt that showed his well-muscled torso—though she already knew about that part from having felt it against her back. Just below the sleeve she caught sight of a tattoo—some sort of swirling design inked on his left biceps. His sandy hair could have used a trim, and something about him gave off an air of modern-day James Dean.

"Um… I…" Wow. He'd really taken her aback. Normally she could converse with people she didn't know—she did it all summer every year at the inn. But then, this had been no customary meeting. Even now that she stood a few feet away, she still felt the heat of his body cocooning her as it had a moment ago.

That was when he shifted his gaze from the shutter to her face, flashing a disarming grin.

That was when she took in the crystalline quality of his eyes, shining on her like a couple of blue marbles, or maybe it was more the perfect clear blue of faraway seas.

That was when she realized…he was younger than her, notably so. But hotter than the day was long. And so she gave up trying to speak entirely and settled on just letting a quiet sigh echo out, hoping her unbidden reactions to him didn't show.

Need to know what happens next?
Find out when you order your copy of
The One Who Stays *by Toni Blake,*
available August 2019 wherever you buy your books!

www.Harlequin.com

Love Harlequin romance?

DISCOVER.

Be the first to find out about promotions,
news and exclusive content!

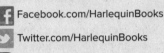

Facebook.com/HarlequinBooks

Twitter.com/HarlequinBooks

Instagram.com/HarlequinBooks

Pinterest.com/HarlequinBooks

ReaderService.com

EXPLORE.

Sign up for the Harlequin e-newsletter and
download a free book from any series at
TryHarlequin.com.

CONNECT.

Join our Harlequin community to share
your thoughts and connect with other
romance readers!
Facebook.com/groups/HarlequinConnection

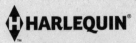

**ROMANCE WHEN
YOU NEED IT**

HSOCIAL201